KILLING EVIL

JOHN NICHOLL

BLOODHOUND
— BOOKS —

www.bloodhoundbooks.com

Print ISBN 978-1-914614-21-7

ALSO BY JOHN NICHOLL

1

I'm a keeper of secrets: dark secrets, filthy secrets, secrets that eat away at my peace of mind like a wild creature feeding on flesh. Unwelcome thoughts claw to leave my troubled mind, pounding, booming pressure and sound threatening to explode my fragile skull into a thousand jagged pieces. Destructive memories of the not-so-distant past, desperate to escape at almost any cost.

I think I've reached that time. An hour I thought may never come. The moment to speak out, to pour out my deep anxiety and dread, to tell you everything, to hold nothing back, whatever the potential consequences for my life. It's something I need to do. Something I *have* to do. I know that now. I no longer have a choice.

Are you ready to read on? Have I captured your interest even slightly? I guess the answer must be yes if you're still reading. I sincerely hope my story doesn't keep you awake at night, as it does me. I've no investment in the discomfort of others, or at least not that of the innocent. You may find my tale shocking. There's no avoiding the horror. But I make no apologies for that.

I can't erase the past. If I'm going to tell you my story, it has to be all of it.

I've experienced terrible things. And I've done awful things too. Some of which you may think are justified, and others perhaps not. Things have a way of running away with themselves. I sometimes went further than even I intended. I can't pretend otherwise. I've committed to total honesty. I'll leave it to you to judge my degree of guilt. All I can offer is mitigation. But try to be kind. Put yourself in my place if you can. Try to be understanding. And I'll try to keep my writing as succinct as possible in return. I'm an enthusiastic reader, a lover of word games. But I won't let emotion cloud the picture. I won't let tears soil the page.

Have we got a deal? Can we shake on it, in a metaphorical sense, without actually meeting? Well, yes or no, I've got my laptop at the ready. So, I'm going to get on with it. I've put it off long enough. Now we get to the heart of the story – the foundation of all that came next.

2

'Sticks and stones may break my bones. But words shall never hurt me.'

The familiar linguistic rhyme came to mind as I cast my thoughts back to my childhood, vivid memories, reliving events as if in real-time. I guess the author's words were well-intentioned. I'm sure the writer meant no malice. But don't believe a word of it, that's my cautionary advice. Words have power; they can hurt; they can control. And they did me to the nth degree.

Words served my father's purpose all too well, as he indulged his deviant tastes with no concern for my well-being, despite my tender years. The *bastard*! I still hate him with a burning intensity I can never hope to erase. Forgiveness? Forget it! He brought nothing but misery to this world, nothing but pain, nothing but suffering. And he did it simply because it pleased him to do so, because he could. Because he thought he could get away with it, that he'd never be caught and punished. Those were all the reasons the pig needed. The *total fucking bastard*! *Ahhhh!* The man was a parasite. I think that's a fair description, although no single word could fully capture his vile

3

persona. He oozed destructive evil. It seeped from every rotten pore of his body. But he hid it from the world; he wore the mask well. Only I saw the bleak reality. He thought of no one but himself.

I was just four years old when it all started; certainly no older than five. I was a young child; an innocent in a dangerous world. I should have been protected in my parents' care. Home should have been a sanctuary, a haven, a place of safety where I could thrive. But it was so very far from that. If heaven can be a place on earth, then so can hell.

I'm not going to focus on that time of my life with any great intensity. It's far too painful. But I'll give you a flavour of events in the interests of understanding. I'll open a window just wide enough for you to glance in. I'm sure you'll get the gist quickly enough if you haven't already done so. It's not as if it's difficult to comprehend. The man was a predator and I his prey. That sums it up very nicely. I was his plaything and in the worst possible way.

I can feel his dirty hands on me even now as I write these words. I can hear his sing-song voice, the urgency, the accent, the tone.

'This is our special secret, Alice. No one else can ever know what we do together.'

That was one of his favourites. I must have heard those poisonous words at least a thousand times back then. He'd place his very ordinary face only inches from mine, with our foreheads almost touching, hissing his words, his whisky-soaked breath filling my nostrils, making me retch.

'Tell no one, Alice! Do you hear me, girl? You'll be taken away if you speak out, to somewhere awful, somewhere terrible. Somewhere infinitely more horrible than you could ever imagine even in your worst nightmares.'

Another example of his repeated contributions to my

confused anxiety. Inevitably followed by something equally diabolical. Anything to put the fear of God into me. Anything to ensure my silence.

'Oh, dear, can you picture it, Alice? It would all be your fault. You'd never see your poor mother again. Do you want that? Do you? You'll keep your mouth shut if you don't.'

And I'd reply, '*No, no, no*, please, Daddy, *no!*' or something along those lines, swallowing his every lying word, believing every untruth that spewed from his venomous mouth. That's the way it works with adults. Children believe them. And I believed *him*. The bastard understood that. He used it to his advantage for nine long years. He used it because it was easy for him, he knew he could.

I can remember it now as if it were yesterday, his lies ringing in my ears, louder and louder. I'm trembling now as I think about it.

'Tell no one.'

That was a line he often used, repeating it, driving his message home time and again. Anything to keep me silent. Anything to avoid detection. Anything to continue along his destructive path.

'Never tell a single soul. If you did, if you said anything, the consequences would be too terrible to contemplate. You'd break your poor mother's heart. Do you want that? Do you, do you?'

Then, just when I thought it was nearly over, he'd pick up a belt, or a hairbrush, or some other implement with which to beat me, somewhere where it didn't show. Never where it showed. That was part of the subterfuge. He was never careless, always careful, considered. He was practised, his methods honed over time. The bastard knew exactly what he was doing. And he kept doing it, however much I pleaded. However much I wanted it to stop. He hurt me often because he didn't care.

Give me a second. I need to compose myself before

continuing. The memories are closing in, raw, painful, surrounding me mercilessly. If only... if only... Oh, what's the point in even thinking it? It happened. I can't change that... I think I'm ready to go on:

'No, Daddy, no!'

Whack!

I can hear the impact of each stinging blow even now. I can feel it on my skin. I can picture the bruises, red, blue, purple, green, yellow and brown. Once, then again and repeat. That was his usual pattern, as his breathing intensified, like an overheated dog in need of water, his chest rising and falling with the effort of it all. He'd get red in the face, sweaty, panting, then aroused, always aroused. Violence never failed to excite him sexually. For him, that was the point of it all. I'm certain of that as I look back on events now. Although, of course, I didn't understand that at the time.

I'd be crying as he'd hurt me, hushed, as quietly as possible, swallowing my sadness, stifling my girlish sobs, straining my being to try and make it stop.

'The punishment,' he called it. I deserved it, apparently, time and again. And in the end I believed it. That it was my fault just as he said. That I deserved no less.

His face would contort, muscles tensed, contours changing, snarling. 'You're a *bad* girl, *evil*! Do you hear me, Alice? *Evil!* I'll beat the sin out of you. I have to do it. You do know that, don't you? It's not me that's doing it, it's you, it's you: you dirty, bad girl. You drive me to it. You're a filthy temptress sent by the devil. You've brought it on yourself.'

I yearned to say no, to yell no, and keep shouting *no, no, no*, until he finally understood and stopped his abuse of my body, mind and spirit. But where would that have got me? Reason was lost on him. My wasted words would only have made things worse, infinitely worse. I think I always knew that, instinctively, without having to be told. My silence was a means of survival. Until I was old enough to... Until... Until... Well, more of that later. I will come to that part of the story but not quite yet. I mustn't jump ahead. It's not yet that time.

Whack!

He'd hit me again. Harder this time, with force, as he blew out the air, spittle spraying from his mouth.

Whack!

'Stop moving, lie still and shut your mouth. What is wrong with you, girl? You're making this worse for yourself. May God forgive you! It's all down to you. Original sin!'

I'd fight to stop shaking, instantly, without hesitation, my entire body tense, fibrous muscles rigid; his words imprisoning me as effectively as any high prison walls.

'Don't make a sound, not a bleat, not a whimper. Or you'll be sorry. You'll spend an eternity in hell. Do you hear me, girl? *Hell!* It's no more than you deserve.'

I actually thought I may have been in hell for a time. The bastard had a million ways to silence me back then, skilled manipulations that ranged from feigned kindness to threats of brutality that he was only too ready to inflict at even the slightest provocation. I think he lived for those moments when he could harm me. They excited him to the point of orgasm. I could see it in his eyes as I got older, the glee, the thrill. I saw it, but no one else did.

He lived two lives, you see, the fiction and the reality he hid from the world. And he was good at it too. People liked him; they respected him, my father, the black-clad preacher with the contrasting white dog collar he seemed so very proud of. The apparent pillar of the community, the monster hidden in plain sight. He wore the mask well. Now do you get it? I was lost in a sea of despair. Do you understand the predicament in which I found myself? I like to think you can.

I'm going to pause for a second or two... To wipe away a tear... To regain my self-control... The writing process is proving infinitely more difficult than I anticipated... I need to blow my nose... There, that's better. I can breathe more easily now. I'm okay to go on:

I still hear the bastard's words sometimes when I close my eyes, as if whispered in my ear. As if he's still with me after all this time, a dark, haunting spectre refusing to let me rest even for a moment. Hateful words repeated time and again, uttered in the dead of night when sleep is beyond my fitful reach. As if I never escaped his unwelcome clutches, those cold, filthy fingers that stroked or prodded, or poked, inflicting pain in one way or another, physical, psychological and emotional, offering nothing but confusion, nothing but distress.

But I'm not a child anymore. I'm my own woman now, an adult. It's time to break the shackles. Time to shine a bright light into the gloom, to lift the metaphorical stone. Monsters thrive in darkness; they feed on secrets, hungry, ravenous; such things give them their power. And so here you are, my diary, the whole and unfettered truth; or at least my version of it. Others may have a different story to tell. I like to think it's a tale of righteous justice, of my victory over evil, although revenge is perhaps a better word to describe it. I'm not in total denial. I know what I've become. And I accept it too. It's my destiny, my role in life. A strange reality some will find hard to believe. But I can tell you it's true. Every single word of it. I know because it happened to me.

3

I've decided to introduce myself now and be done with it. Anything less would seem impolite. And that's the last thing I'd want. I don't want to give you a poor impression of myself, not at this early stage of my tale. Things are bad enough without unnecessary rudeness. Of course, I won't share my real name, the one I was given at birth. That would be ill-advised, inviting trouble, as you'll come to realise. I'm not the brightest bulb in the box. But I'm not stupid either. I wouldn't have survived this long if I was. I'll call myself Alice Granger for the sake of the story. I think that works well enough. I heard the name somewhere along the way and liked it. I can't remember where, but it serves my purpose.

I'm not expecting you to like me. I'm not out to make friends; that's not my motive. But I do hope you'll understand the extremes to which I've travelled when you fully consider events. I gave you a flavour of my childhood, the things *he* did, the things *he* said. The type of man he was. But I'm not going to dwell on it. Why torture myself? What purpose would it serve? You can fill in the gaps if you choose to.

I'm going to jump forward in time to the day of my thirteenth birthday. I think that makes sense. It was a bitterly cold, winter day with a cloudless pale-blue sky, and a low, bright sun that lit the coal-stained hills behind our semi-detached Victorian home as I looked out from my bedroom window.

I can still remember each moment of that day, the anniversary of my birth. It's imprinted on my mind forever, carved in tablets of stone until my dying day. It was an important day, a causative day, a catalyst that created what I've become. Everything changed that cold winter day. I didn't realise it at the time, not initially, that took time. But as I look back on it now, it seems glaringly obvious. Nothing would ever be the same.

I can remember sitting down for my birthday tea, me, my mother, *that man* all dressed in black, and my baby sister, just three years old, seated in a wooden high chair that had once been mine, looking from one of us to another, smiling, blissfully oblivious to the awful dangers that inhabited her world. And then I saw it. That *man*, the *bastard*, the *monster*, looking at my baby sister as he often looked at me. It was a look I hated, an expression I dreaded, lustful, drooling, an all too reliable predictor of the horrors to come. I knew in that instant that my sister was in terrible danger. The sort of risk I couldn't let her face. I felt a crushing, almost overwhelming responsibility to protect her, to save her from the ravages that my father's unwanted attention would inevitably bring.

I looked first at my father and then at my mother: my tired, worn-out, lacklustre mother, beaten down by life; and I knew without a doubt that she'd seen it too, that look, the monster peeking out from behind his mask. My mother tensed, tight muscles changing the contours of her face. But she didn't say anything; she never said anything, not a single word, or at least nothing meaningful. Nothing that could change anything for the better. I always hoped she would speak up in defence of her daughters, but it never happened, not even once. Denial was her survival tactic. I understand that now. It was a self-therapy of sorts. She raised invisible walls all around herself. High impenetrable walls I couldn't hope to break down any more than she could. I stared at her, trying to meet her eyes, imploring her to speak out, as she averted her gaze to the wall.

I rose with warm tears welling in my eyes, and ran to the small first-floor bathroom, where I threw up until there was nothing left but green, acidic bile. I washed out my mouth with cold water and squirted a small blob of spearmint toothpaste into my open mouth before returning to the kitchen, tears still staining my face. And that was the end of my birthday tea, the party was over. My father silently headed to his garden office, to which he often retreated. And my mother tidied the kitchen, making the place 'look presentable', as she often put it. She wandered around the room as if in a trance, with me mirroring her every step, trying to speak, to *really* speak, from the heart. I wanted her to listen, to take me seriously, to do the right thing.

'*He* did it again last night, Mum. *He* came to my room. *He*–'

She interrupted me. She always interrupted me. I should have got used to it but I never did. 'Come on now, Alice, that's enough of that silly talk. Fetch the plates from the table. There's a good girl. They're not going to wash themselves.'

I just stood there, statue like, not moving an inch, as if welded to the spot. It wasn't the first time I'd attempted to tell her. I'd tried several times over the years. I'd even shown her the bruises. I repeated myself now, louder and more insistently this time, completing my statement despite her turning away. I knew she'd heard. How could she not have? But I may as well have not opened my mouth at all.

My mother's gaze bounced from one part of the room to

another. She was looking at anything but me. And then she finally spoke again, breaking the silence, high-pitched, urgent, desperate to silence me, a look of virtual panic on her face. 'Now look what you've done, your sister's crying. You are so ungrateful for your many blessings. I made you a nice cake with candles. Why spoil what's been a lovely day?'

I wasn't going to give up that easily.

'What if he turns on Sarah next? Have you thought about that? Because he will, he definitely will. You saw the way he looked at her, just like I did.'

Silence, other than my sister whimpering to my left.

'Didn't you hear me, Mother? Didn't you hear what I said to you?'

She'd heard all right, of course she had, like every other time I'd spoken out. But it made no difference. She picked Sarah up, headed towards the hall, up the stairs, and into her bedroom at the back of the house, where she closed the door against the world.

I was alone. My mother wouldn't listen, and I didn't believe anyone else would either. I'm sure now that wasn't true. But it seemed that way to me. I'd once tried talking to a church elder, who'd simply told my father what I'd said, unbelieving, unable or unwilling to help. I was seen as the problem both within the family home and the church I'd attended all my life. I was the wayward child, a burden to my parents, a girl in need of counselling and prayer, their cross to bear. It was a more naive time when many people found it hard to believe that a significant number of men posed a serious risk to children: children like me.

As I lay awake in my single bed that night, jumping at even the slightest sound, afraid of shadows, fearful of *his* hand on the door handle, I came to a realisation. If my sister was to be safe, my father had to die. That's the conclusion I came to at the age of thirteen. And I believed it too. I still believe it with every part of my being. There was no other option. It shouldn't have been that way, but it was. The bastard couldn't be allowed to live for a day longer than necessary. It didn't really matter how he died, as long as he did. As unlikely as it seemed, I was going to find a way of putting him in the ground. I just had to work out how.

4

My father's much-loved garden office was invaded by rats the following March, which pleased me more than I can say. The odious man had left various tempting foodstuffs readily available after a drunken night of whisky excess. And so the opportunistic little rodents had gnawed their way through the structure's wooden floor with those prominent front teeth of theirs, before filling their bellies at my father's expense.

I liked that! I liked it a lot. I can't stress that sufficiently. It was more than a simple act of nature. It told me that *he* wasn't all-powerful. That he had his vulnerabilities like everybody else. Nature had thrown him a curveball. For all his prayers, God wasn't on his side. I took comfort in the fact that some things were beyond the bastard's control. And soon, I would be too. I said it and almost believed it. I was desperate to believe it. I repeated it in my head time and again for only me to hear. In a short time, his world would come crashing down. If he thought the rats were a problem, there was much more to come. His reluctant plaything had become his nemesis, an agent of divine punishment. A flaming sword of vengeance and justice hung above his head in my mind's eye. I wanted him dead. I had never hated anyone more.

I can clearly remember the bastard's outraged reaction, as he paced around the kitchen table, his face reddening, tiny beads of sweat forming on his brow. He was going to kill the rats, every single one of them. He yelled words to that effect as he searched for his car keys, and then he left the house, slamming the front door behind him so hard that it shook in its frame. He returned about half an hour or so later with several large, shiny steel traps, and two white plastic containers of poisonous, blue-stained grain. He held one of the two plastic receptacles up in plain sight for both myself and my mother to see.

'This will put an end to the little swines! How dare they? Have you seen the state of the floor? It's a complete disgrace.'

My mother forced an unconvincing smile, hugging my little sister while confirming that she had indeed seen the floor, and uttering words of encouragement to shut him up. And I tried to fade into the background while they talked, making myself smaller, and watching from a safe distance as his anger intensified.

If the poison could kill the rats, it could kill him too. That's what I told myself, less than convincingly. It could, couldn't it, if he ingested enough? Maybe this was the answer I was looking for – the key to my plight, and my sister's too. A resolution delivered direct to our door. Maybe it was fate, already written, the Creator's will. Or perhaps it was me, just me alone, searching for meaning, for reassurance in a frightening world.

I followed my father out into our back garden, with its multicoloured spring flowers bordering the manicured lawn. But I didn't see the beauty. It didn't register even for a moment. I was focused on *him* and only him, as he often was on me with all the horrors that held. I stood at a distance, well out of his reach, but close enough to watch as he administered the poison, dropping several heaped spoonfuls of the blue-stained grain into the uneven hole in the wooden floor.

I stayed in the garden after he returned to the house, muttering as he went. I considered my next step, thoughts spinning in my head, weighing up my options. I experienced a heady mix of excitement and fear as adrenalin surged through my bloodstream, flight or fight but with nowhere to run. I knew I had to poison him, but how? That was the question, how?

I walked around the edge of the lawn, glancing from one window to another, up, down, from left to right and back again, hoping no one could read my thoughts. And then it came to me in a blinding flash of inspiration. Why not feign a new interest in cooking? That could work. I could help my mother with the family's feeding and poison a meal when the opportunity arose. Yes, that seemed like a good idea. Perhaps a meaty stew or a hot curry with rice, something that would adequately mask the blue grain well enough for him to digest it in sufficient quantity. I'd have to ensure no one else ate any of the contaminated food, of course, that was essential. But I could do it, couldn't I? If I used the right curry powder blend with extra chilli. If I held my nerve. Neither my mother nor my baby sister was fond of spicy food. I could use that to my advantage. Yes, the hotter the better!

The bastard would gulp it down like the greedy pig he was. He'd be dead in minutes, nothing but a memory, rotting in hell. I pictured events as I lay in bed that night and decided to act at the first opportunity. It was more than a female fantasy. I was going to do it. The decision was made. There was no going back.

I was both gratified and a little apprehensive when my mother encouraged my new-found interest in cooking in the coming days. It surprised but pleased her. I think that's a fair summary of her reaction. And I was gaining confidence as my plan approached fruition. My father hadn't changed, of course. Men like him never do. He still invaded my room at night when it suited him. And his interest in my little sister was growing as she approached her fourth birthday. I pleaded with him to leave her alone, but he just smiled thinly without parting his lips and walked away as if I'd said nothing at all. I knew only too well what was coming. It was up to me to save her. And I was running out of time. I've said it before and I'll say it again: if heaven can be a place on earth, then so can hell.

I decided the time had come. I couldn't put it off any longer. It was all arranged. I was to cook a family meal the following Friday evening after school. Stew for the rest of us and curry for him. All I had to do was use two pots – one with spices and one without. Prawn vindaloo was my father's favourite meal, and hopefully, his last. Although it seemed the rats had taken a little longer to die. That shocked me at first. Death took a bit of time and effort. Father administered the blue grain several times before the desperately thirsty creatures finally passed. It seemed the rats had become resistant to the toxic chemical. Here was hoping it was different with humans. I realised I might have to repeat the process, too. There may be other meals to cook and contaminate. I had to hold my nerve.

Friday evening couldn't come quickly enough. I was like a happy child anticipating a Christmas morning. Mother has sourced all the necessary ingredients from the local supermarket, and I was mentally prepared. I'd pictured events in my head. I'd celebrated his death in my imagination. Now all I had to do was create that happy reality. I was ready to go, nerves jangling, but still determined.

And then it happened. Something unexpected, a complication I hadn't considered even for a moment. My mother and father sat at the kitchen table that evening as I began cooking, and talked of a neighbour's unexpected death. The poor woman was only in her early forties. A seemingly healthy wife and mother who often exercised, so full of life. As bad as that was, it wasn't my neighbour's premature demise that shocked and concerned me so very much. There was going to be a post-mortem. The authorities would find out *exactly* how and why she died.

My legs stiffened as I stood at the range cooker. I met my mother's tired eyes across the room and asked the inevitable question. 'Is there always a post-mortem after someone's death?'

I think I knew the answer long before she opened her mouth to speak. My mother nodded twice, her head moving in jerks. She was tense as always, as if on full alert. Keen to answer, anything but silence. 'Yes, yes, there is, if the death is unexpected, or the cause is unknown. That's right, isn't it, George?'

It was my father's turn to nod this time, pompous, full of himself, always the expert on everything, as he poured himself another whisky, the third in a matter of minutes. He drained his glass before answering, making her wait. He always did that. It gave him power. 'Yes, it's a very necessary process. Best not to think about it at teatime. It's all part of God's great plan.'

That may or may not be the case. But what I do know is that my plan was torn to pieces in that instant. My gut twisted as my legs buckled, the room becoming an impressionist blur as I sank to the tiled floor.

I was lost in a sea of despair for weeks on end after that. All my hopes were dashed. I felt hopeless, more hopeless than ever before. It seemed my father was in control after all. I cried often and struggled to eat. My mother wanted me to see a doctor. To have a medical, to be checked out. But Father was never going to let that happen, not in a million years. I could have said something. I may have spoken out. I had before so why not again? And so the bastard placated my mother with offers of prayers. I'm sure she knew exactly what he was doing. But she went along with it. She always gave in, folding under whatever pressure he inflicted; anything for an easier life. Mother was a shadow of a woman, manipulated, isolated, and controlled. And he was good at it too, something of a master. It's how he facilitated his continued offending, how he fed his grotesque and deviant needs. I can see that now through my more experienced eyes. I can see it as clear as day. His word was law, his and his alone. He was the god in our house, and my mother turned a blind eye, broken, defeated, anything to help her cope for one more day.

I may well have harmed myself in those dark days, had it not been for my sister. I certainly considered it – anything to bring my unhappy reality to an end. I thought of little else at times. But suicide is never the answer. Cling onto hope, that's my advice. There's often a light at the end of that very dark tunnel. I'd almost given up on any expectation of redemption when an unexpected opportunity arose, without any need for planning.

Give me a second. My mouth's a little parched. I'll fetch a glass of water to oil the creative wheels. And then I'll tell you what happened next.

Okay, my throat's eased, my thirst quenched, and so here we go again. I really like this part of my story. I can feel my spirits rising in anticipation of the telling. You may or may not feel the same.

My father liked walking, which meant we walked a great distance and often. He frequently took us on long country treks in the spring and summer. And the April in question was no different once the Easter church services were over. My sister was dropped off at my maternal grandmother's nearby home, after which we headed to the beautiful seaside county of Pembrokeshire in our aged, faded-red estate car, which had long since seen better days.

We must have looked like an ordinary family to anyone who cared to look, unremarkable, not particularly surprising or different from the happy norm. But first impressions can be notoriously unreliable.

I was dreading the day because I'd spend it with *him* – the man who offered nothing but misery. He spoilt everything by being the man he was, by being there, by existing, simply by drawing breath. He was a dark cloud who shaped my childhood experience. A poison chalice from which I was forced to drink.

We left the car on a convenient grass verge at the side of a country road, and headed off towards Cemaes Head – with its spectacular high granite cliffs rising majestically from the sea. And that's where it happened. In that glorious place of infinite beauty. God's creation at its very best.

We'd been walking along the narrow stone-strewn path for about half an hour or so when Father suddenly stopped to peer over the edge of the cliff at something or other in the blue-green sea far below. Mother trudged on as he stood there, teetering only inches from the edge, holding his binoculars to his eyes seemingly without a care in the world.

And then I did it, instinctively, without a moment's thought. I crept up behind him one step at a time, ever so slowly, ever so carefully, my heart pounding so very loudly that I feared he might hear it. But my fears were unfounded. I kept moving, one step, two steps, then another, then another. And then I threw myself forward when I thought the time was exactly right. I used all my weight and strength to send him sprawling, flailing in mid-air as if trying to fly, as he plunged over 500 feet to the cold and unforgiving water below.

Brief seconds passed like minutes as he tumbled, seemingly in slow motion, until he hit a large, jagged rock only inches below the sea's surface. Dark blood poured from a head wound, mixing with the salty water and then washing away. I knew that it was finally over. My sister was safe. I was free of him. It was a glorious moment. A celebration of my will to survive and conquer. Now all I had to do was get away with it. That was as important as the act itself. It was then and it is now. Punishment was never a part of the plan.

I felt no remorse, no guilt or regret, as I called after my mother, who was now about twenty metres away, still walking on along the cliff path. I bit my tongue hard, drawing blood, forcing tears as she looked back, puzzlement on her face. And then she asked the question I'd been dreading, her tone almost monotone, bordering on the melancholy. 'Where on earth has your father gone?'

I pointed down towards the sea with a finger that wouldn't stop shaking. 'He fell! He– he was close to the edge, and– and he fell. There was nothing– nothing I could do.'

She appeared more animated now, her voice rising in pitch and volume, demanding to be heard above the sea breeze. 'He fell?'

I pointed again as she walked towards me. 'Yes, yes, he fell, over the edge, right down there into the sea. And he– he hit a rock.' I thrust out my hand to show her. 'That rock. Can you see it, the one below the water? I tried to grab him, but I was– I was too slow. One second he was there, and then he wasn't. There was nothing I could do.'

Was that the hint of a smile on my mother's face as she rushed towards me? I like to think it was. She hugged me tightly for what seemed like an age before finally dropping to all fours and crawling to the cliff edge, peering over with keen eyes. But my father's body was nowhere to be seen, carried away by the tide. Mother seemed strangely unemotional as she looked back at me, reversing, still on all fours for a few seconds longer, before finally rising. She took my hand and sat me down on the far side of the path, away from the cliff edge, before sitting herself, with our shoulders touching. It felt good, reassuring, as we sat together in silence, watching the soaring gulls, listening to the wind, appreciating the sun on our faces. Neither of us said a single word until she finally uncrossed her legs, taking her smartphone from a trouser pocket about five minutes later. She dialled 999, asked for the coastguard, and then we sat in renewed silence as we waited for the emergency services.

5

After my father's death, Mother seemed more relaxed once the inevitable formalities related to tragic accidents were finally over. The authorities didn't suspect a thing. We were just a seemingly ordinary family out for a long walk on a warm spring day in the Welsh sunshine. My father went too close to the edge, he slipped, he lost his balance and then he fell. It really was as simple as that. That's what I told anyone who was interested. I made a written statement to that effect on the day of his death. I'm not saying it was easy to lie to the police, and there were anxieties, I can't deny that. My stomach was doing somersaults. But a part of me enjoyed the subterfuge. I knew something no one else knew. And that made me feel important. It made me feel powerful for the first time in my life, a winner. I wouldn't say I like admitting to that fact. It's not something I'm proud of. But it's how it was.

I recall the young female police officer looking me in the eye with what seemed like genuine sympathy. I can even remember her name, PC Heather Kemp. That sticks in my mind because I liked her. She was kind, gentle, oblivious to my trickery. Why would she suspect a young girl had executed her preacher father? Would anyone? I think most would say Heather was good at her job.

'Are you all right to go on, Alice?'

I looked back across the interview room's table at the young policewoman's friendly face, wiping a tear from my eye with one hand while clutching my mother's wrist with the other. I hurried my words. Keen to move things along and get out of there before I slipped up or the officer started asking questions that were difficult to answer. 'Yes, yes, I think I'd rather get it over with.'

Mother placed a supportive arm around my shoulders as I waited for whatever came next. She was the next to speak. That surprised me. I was expecting her to sit there in virtual silence. She rarely said anything at all. 'The poor girl's in shock.'

That amused me no end, my mother's stated opinion of my state of mind. I found it hard not to laugh. She really couldn't have been more wrong. But the uniformed officer nodded her acknowledgement, seemingly in full agreement, shifting in her seat as if unable to get comfortable. I was there as a witness, not a suspect, I realise that now. And that was crucial. Had I been a suspect, things would have been very different.

'Are you sure you don't want to take a break, Alice? It wouldn't be a problem. There's no rush. Would you like something to drink, perhaps, a glass of water or squash? We can take as long as you need.'

I lowered my gaze, speaking quietly, my eyes narrowed to slits. I was enjoying the interview more by that stage. I was feeling more relaxed as I shaped events. Comfortable in my own skin. The nice officer was eating out of my hand. It was going better than I could ever have hoped. It seemed I could lie almost as well as my father. I'd learnt from the master. It was time to drive home my advantage. 'I'm not thirsty, thank you, Heather.

Dad went too near the edge of the cliff and then he fell, there's no more to say. That's exactly as it happened. I saw it all.'

The officer tapped her yellow plastic pen on the tabletop three times. 'Okay, if you're sure you're okay to go on, we'll continue. You're doing really well... Did your father say anything at all before he fell?'

I choked back a smile that threatened to betray me at the worst possible time. I think a part of her was wondering if he'd jumped. Or maybe she just needed to rule that out. Yes, that was probably it. Dot the i's and cross the t's. I didn't need to lie now. I just told PC Kemp the truth. Or, at least, I told her the part of it I wanted her to hear. The story I *needed* her to hear. And she listened. She swallowed every single word of it. I was a conductor, directing the orchestra of events, shaping the young officer's perception of reality as I chose. That taught me something important. When questioned, it's best to stick as close to the truth as possible without actually implicating yourself. It's easier that way. It reduces the risk, and that's a good thing that's well worth pursuing. And so I told my tale, right up to the point I sent the evil bastard tumbling to his death on the rocks below. That was the one bit I left out.

'One moment Dad was standing there looking through his binoculars, and then he wasn't. He didn't say a word. And he didn't scream either. I don't know why. I'm sure I would have. Maybe he didn't want to frighten me. That's the only explanation I can think of.'

The officer began making written notes in blue scribbled script. 'And you saw all of that happen? That's what you're telling me, yes?'

I nodded once, then again, slowly, lowering my head, staring down at the desktop, resisting the temptation to giggle. I sank my teeth into my tongue again and winced, a snigger becoming a pained cry. Not only had I seen it happen. I'd *made* it happen, me, me, me! I was so very proud of that. But, of course, I was never going to admit that, not then, not to her. I spoke through my tears. I had a mask too. Father had taught me well.

'Yes, I saw it, all of it, exactly as I've told you. It's the worst thing I've ever seen. It broke my heart. I loved Daddy so very much.'

PC Kemp paused momentarily before speaking again. I still don't know why she stalled as she did. I asked myself if I'd gone too far, perhaps I'd said too much. But, no, all was well. The nice officer smiled again as she reached out, gently patting my hand. 'Okay, Alice, thank you for telling me everything that you saw. I know it can't have been easy for you. You've been a *very* brave girl. Now, let's get a statement down on paper, and then you and your mum can get off home. I'll write everything you've told me down, and then you can read and sign it as a true record of events. How does that sound? Do you understand? Is that okay with you?'

I knew she was trying to be kind. Three questions in one. She wanted it over with. And that suited me just fine. I did exactly as the nice officer suggested, and that was it. Things really couldn't have gone any better. PC Kemp wrote down my fictional version of events, and I scribbled my signature as required, confirming it was nothing but the truth. I couldn't quite believe it was that easy, but it was, it really was. It was as if my dreams were coming true.

As I walked away from the police station, hand in hand with my mother later that day, I had an undoubted skip in my step. I wanted to leap and bound and dance and yell out my triumph. But I hid it well. I looked up at the cloudless blue sky as a wave of elation made my entire body tingle. I'd never felt such energy, such joy. My long-time tormentor was dead, and my world was a

26

better place. A safer place for me and my sister too. I hadn't forgiven my mother for her failure to protect me, not yet, not totally, it was far too soon for that. But maybe such things would come. It was time to focus on the positives; one of the happiest moments of my life.

6

My father's bruised and battered body was found washed up on a remote north Pembrokeshire beach by an unfortunate dog walker a few days later, and identified using his dental records.

My mother never saw the corpse. It was too far gone for that. And I feel sure that suited her just fine. She'd been a very different woman since his death, as if a weight had been lifted from her. There were a few tears from time to time. But I got the distinct impression they were tears of relief rather than sadness. I almost told her the truth of what I'd done more than once. But even then I suspected it was a burden she wasn't strong enough to bear. And so I kept it to myself, *my* special secret. Mother was still fragile. I felt no remorse or regret. So my continued silence seemed to make sense. Secrecy was best. My opinion hasn't changed in the years since. I still put her feelings first in that regard. Why upset her unnecessarily? What could it possibly achieve? And so I'm kind like that officer. I think I learnt that from her. Now, that's something I am proud of. There's goodness in me despite everything I've done. I'm not devoid of virtue.

My mother arranged a cremation, despite my father having

requested burial in the churchyard with which he was so familiar. Mother told me that herself. He'd made his expectations perfectly clear. Not just orally but in writing: his instructions were included in his will. He'd specified the burial, the words on a headstone, even the service's details were outlined as if he was anticipating death despite his relative youth. But my mother chose to ignore his instructions. She could do it after his death but sadly not before. It was her spark of rebellion. She'd spent *years* doing exactly what he commanded in that overbearing, bullying way of his. And now she was free of him and his harsh words. Free like those glorious, swooping gulls we watched that day on the magnificent Pembrokeshire cliff edge, as we sat in silence, bonded in hardship.

After a brief, well-attended service at the church where Father had so recently been the vicar, Mother drove the twenty or so miles to the crematorium with me sitting alongside her in the front passenger seat of the car. She'd received numerous offers to provide the transport, but she'd politely declined. I never thought to ask why. I don't know what she really thought or felt that day or since. We don't ask, do we? We assume or give the ideas and opinions of others little or no thought at all, even those close to us when focused on ourselves, as I was on the day. I'll put it down to the self-focus of youth.

My sister was left in the care of her paternal grandmother, who attended the church service but not the cremation. That didn't seem strange to me at the time. But now I wonder if she knew something of her second son's true nature. I never asked her then, and I still haven't to this day.

I remember standing outside the crematorium, hand in hand with my mother, sheltering under a slanted, Welsh slate roof which protected the main entrance as the rain began to fall. The rain got gradually heavier as we stood there in silence, as if God were mourning humanity's many failings and frailties. I remember my mother squeezing my hand once, then again, as six adult male bearers of various ages, all of whom were members of Father's church, lifted the dark-oak coffin from the back of the hearse, supporting it on their shoulders, taking the strain. We followed on slowly as they carried the coffin into the building to a familiar hymn, which Mother later told me was a favourite of hers, but not *his*. That told its own story, but of course, those in attendance were unaware of her rebellion. I had my secrets, and so did my mother. No one else needed to know.

We sat at the front of the room, along with other close relatives, and waited as the wooden pews filled behind us, one at a time. The service started at eleven o'clock sharp, the combination of English and Welsh hymns, prayers and readings coming to a timely end about half an hour later, as Father's coffin entered the burning flames.

I pictured him inside that wooden box, and that was it, it was done. It really felt over now. I'd never see the bastard again except in my flashbacks and nightmares. I was under no misapprehension on that score. Those didn't leave me despite his demise, not completely. They've faded over the years, their sting less sharp, but I doubt they'll ever go away completely. That's why I'm writing these words to exorcise the past. I'm sure you understand that. It's a remedy of sorts. Something I have to do. It's a way of nailing my father's coffin tight shut. Maybe then, when I've finished, I won't hear him opening my bedroom door anymore. He still does sometimes. I see him. He whispers in my ear.

Twenty or more people joined us back at the house after the cremation service, to drink tea or coffee, eat pre-prepared sandwiches, and extol my father's virtues, as if he'd actually been a good man, some kind of saint if such a thing exists. They didn't see the monster I'd experienced behind closed doors from such a young age. He wore his mask well even after his death.

Listening to those ill-informed words of praise for a man I detested was hard to bear. I wanted to retreat to the garden, to not hear their nonsense, to celebrate his end privately, and to be alone with my thoughts. Or better still, to tell them exactly what he'd been.

He was a monster! A stinking, filthy, predatory monster and I his victim! He wasn't the man you thought you knew. He put his dirty hands on me from the age of four, that devil in human form.

I pictured the scene in my mind as if it were real. If only! Can you imagine their reaction had I acted on my impulse? A part of me wanted to shout it out, to yell it for everyone to hear. And to keep shouting until his grovelling devotees finally believed it. For however long it took to shatter their illusions. But even then I knew that continued deceit was the only way forward. And so I played the grieving daughter with some aplomb, thanking them for their words of kindness, conveying my sadness, acting the heartbroken child grieving my terrible loss. And I convinced them, I'm certain of that. They saw what I needed them to see. It was something I was good at, a skill that would serve me well over time. It still does now.

I didn't know then that further deception was to come as the years passed. Those dark days were the start of something, not the end. My father wasn't the only monster in existence. There were others out there in this big bad world of ours. Deviant, manipulative, predacious monsters in need of slaying. Not mythical creatures, but men, dangerous men who live amongst us. They often put themselves in positions of trust to gain easy access to children. The devious *bastards*! But more of that later, I've said enough for now. We'll come to it in good time. I'm tired in body and spirit.

It's a time for rest. Now, where is that sleeping medication? I know it's here somewhere, my chemical cosh in a plastic bottle. Ah, yes, there it is. I've found it, in a drawer amongst the knives. I'll wash the syrup down with a little alcohol, vodka maybe, or even a whisky. And so bye for now, welcome oblivion beckons. I need to lay my head on the pillow. It's a Saturday tomorrow, so no work for me. I'll tell you what happened next when I wake in the morning.

7

Living in *that house* wasn't easy, even after my father's death. The bastard's dark shadow was everywhere, the memories too vivid, too bright, too loud, and too powerful. It was as if he was still with me at times. As if he'd never died. But he was dead. I knew that better than most. I'd seen it happen. I'd *made* it happen. I'd done it, me; I was the winner and my father the loser. For all his manipulative power I'd destroyed him that day on the clifftop. I reminded myself of that incessantly. I'd picture him falling through mid-air in those times of distress, raising my spirits, remembering and reinforcing my ultimate triumph, good over evil.

Either that or I'd recall his wooden coffin entering the burning fire in that small country crematorium to the sound of a hymn he hadn't appreciated in life. I'd picture his body engulfed in scorching flames, his spirit travelling on its final journey to hell.

And my recollections worked to a degree. His shadow retreated for a time, before returning in my weaker moments when I was weary or lowered my guard. I wanted to leave home, to live anywhere else but there. And who could blame me? I suggested a house move for the family, a new start somewhere else entirely, to somewhere offering fresh opportunities without reminders of the past. It would have made absolute sense for all of us, not just for me, but for my mother and sister too. We all needed new horizons in which to recover and grow in the absence of ghosts.

But my mother had different ideas. She'd used my father's life insurance settlement to pay off what was left of the mortgage. She'd taken his many possessions to various local charity shops in black plastic bin bags. And she'd redecorated almost every room in the house in a frenzy of activity, replacing the carpets and much of the furniture, my bed included. She burnt my old bed in the back garden no doubt thinking that was enough to rectify the past. As if those physical changes had somehow eradicated all that had gone before. As if the many horrors witnessed by those stone walls had never happened.

In summary, my mother didn't think a house move was necessary however much I argued the point. She said it and repeated it despite my arguments to the contrary. I think it may have been because she wanted to be near my maternal grandmother. But a move was needed, it so was. The refurbishments may have been enough for her, but they certainly weren't for me. I still saw the monster from time to time, lurking in the shadows in the dead of night, ready to pounce, to run his filthy hands over my skin. And so I resolved to leave that house of bad memories at the earliest opportunity. A new life beckoned as my teenage years progressed, which gave me a hope that I clung onto with every part of my being. I planned to move away to study. That was my escape plan, my way out. Soon I'd be on my way. I could embrace change. I wasn't stuck there forever. A new life was possible. And hooray to that.

I achieved eight reasonably good GCSE grades, an A, two Bs and five Cs, and then went on to study art, computer studies and history at A-level in the sixth form at the same school. I liked the computer work the best. It captured my attention and kept me focused. It stopped me thinking more than was good for me. And I was reasonably good at it too. Or, at least, I like to think so. My teacher said as much more than once.

But my results at the end of the two-year course weren't nearly good enough for me to go on to study for a university degree in the pleasant Welsh capital Cardiff, as I'd intended. That was crushing at first. I was so very disappointed that I almost gave up.

My mother suggested resits, a logical response on the face of it. But that would have meant delaying the changes I so desperately needed. I should have worked harder. I could have revised more before the exams that meant so very much. But I didn't. How stupid was that? I could hear my father saying it, shouting it in my ear as if he was there in the room. He mocked me even after his death.

A new plan was necessary if I was going to escape my private hell. I had no option but to lower my academic aspirations. College rather than university seemed a viable alternative. And so I filled in the online forms and applied for a college degree course, much to my mother's anxiety and dismay. She objected at first, insisting university was best for a girl of my academic abilities and promise. But she soon relented when I explained that it was something I *had* to do. It wasn't a matter of choice; it was a case of necessity. I had to get out of there. My mental health depended on it. Another day in that house was a day too many. I needed change and fast. I told her that insistently with feeling. And to my surprise and relief, my mother understood almost immediately, as my mood darkened. She didn't push it.

That's how she dealt with things: avoidance, denial, looking away to protect her sanity. My father had beaten her down over time. He drained her resources. My mother was fragile. She's still fragile. An open and honest conversation would be too much for her.

I left home a few days before my first term at a college in a small town about a twenty-minute drive from where I'd grown up. I could have gone further, and maybe I should have, but I still lacked confidence. Maybe Cardiff would have been too much for me after all. But leaving my village to live in a different area, however familiar, seemed like a good idea. There would be other students I knew. People from school. Not all would be strangers. I don't think I could have coped with much more. They weren't friends: I didn't have friends, not real ones, and I still don't. But I'd recognise their faces which offered some comfort.

I'd found a reasonably comfortable, cheap bedsit in a shared building about a fifteen-minute walk from the college campus, which I thought would suit me well enough as I started my new life of independence. Mother said she was happy to help me with my living costs until I found a part-time job to pay the bills. I know it was generous of her, but I still think it was the least she could do given her past failures. She still had a fair amount of insurance money left after a large payout, and she seemed pleased to use it for my benefit. I think that suited both of us. It facilitated my move and assuaged her guilt. I was grateful for the assistance and readily accepted. I still don't think it was selfish. Something positive had come out of my father's death, maybe the only positive thing he'd ever accomplished. I think he'd have hated that.

I was leaving my mother and younger sister to live alone in that big house so full of memories I'd rather forget. And I was fine with that. I'd done my bit. I feel certain I saved my sister from my father's unwelcome advances. She was safe: I'd acted just in time. And so I suspect she was reasonably happy in that house. Her memories were untainted, so unlike my own. The monster only haunted the place for me.

My mother had traded in my father's old, faded estate car for a newer but smaller German hatchback, a sporty model she said she loved to drive. That seemed so unlike her; she was evolving, slowly putting the past behind her, although there were still obvious weaknesses. Those weaknesses are still there, emotional scars every bit as deep as mine. Sadness ages a person. It sucks the life force out of them. It certainly has her. I suspect it's the same for me.

We loaded the car with everything that an independent girl could need, and the three of us travelled together to the town where I'd study.

My mother did her best to put on a brave face as we emptied the car. But I could see her unhappiness. Her eyes were moist and reddening as a single tear ran down her cheek before finding a home on her green cotton collar.

Within an hour, the three of us were sitting in my room, drinking cups of tea from matching pottery mugs bought at a local market. I felt nervous but relieved to be there. I'd done it, I was free, and I couldn't wait for my mother and sister to be on their way.

I stood on the narrow pavement outside my new lodgings about twenty minutes later, waving as they drove off. And that was it. I turned away when the car left my sight.

My plans had come to fruition. My new life had begun. It was more a relief than anything else. I intended to keep in touch with them from time to time, but not to visit unless it was unavoidable. I hoped never to enter *that house* ever again. I thought I could forget. I was that naive in those days. If only it were that simple!

A new journey had started. But it would ultimately take me

on a darker and more perilous path than I could ever have imagined. The past follows us. It creeps up on us when we least suspect it. You'll learn about it as my story continues.

8

My Applied Computing degree course was both challenging and surprisingly enjoyable. My skills developed quickly under my lecturers' expert guidance, which unknown to me, would serve my true calling well in the years to come. I didn't know then that my life had a God-given purpose. That the truly awful experiences of my childhood had shaped me to that specific end. That my father's death was the start of something very much bigger. I hope you'll come to see that too, as my story develops. Everything I've done was beyond my control. I was being rushed along by an irresistible tide.

I kept myself to myself for the most part while studying. Actually, that's understating the case; I avoided meaningful relationships at almost any cost, that's the truth of it. I already knew several of the other students when I first started my BSc studies, and, of course, I got to know others to a superficial extent as the months passed. But I kept those relationships at arm's length, as I had at school, and as I do now. The other undergraduates were friendly enough. My emotional isolation was my choice, as opposed to theirs. You see, I really thought my childhood experience had been unique. I believed that nobody else could possibly understand what I'd been through at the hands of that monster in human form. And trust was an issue too, for obvious reasons I'm certain I don't need to explain. I talked to people when I needed to; when it was unavoidable or to my benefit. I made small talk as necessary but no more than that.

Relationships apart, the course went well. I received good grades in my assignments and I felt increasingly confident of passing my degree at the end of the three years. I hadn't really thought beyond that point. I was trying to live in the moment without much success. But I was reliably informed that the qualification would provide me with a wide range of employment opportunities in both the public and private sectors. And that statement would prove prophetic. I can see that now as I look back on events with a critical eye. Fate was taking me in a direction I couldn't possibly comprehend. Everything would come together as it was supposed to. It was much more than coincidence, a plan written in the stars. I was born for a reason. I have a purpose I have no choice but to fulfil. That's the way it is: sometimes, as God pulls the strings.

More monster men would die as the years passed – beasts like my father, creators of pain, misery and distress. I'll tell you more about that later in my tale.

From year two of the course, I paid my living costs by working most evenings and weekends as a minimum-wage barmaid in a working-class backstreet pub. The majority of the punters were pleasant enough. I occasionally had to put up with misogynistic crap from one drunken idiot or another who fancied their chances, but I was used to a lot worse. And anyway, I was just glad to be free, in body if not entirely in spirit. Does that make any sense in your very different world? Moving on was one thing. But shadows of the past are far more difficult to shake off. Memories follow us for good or bad, creeping, lingering, hiding in the shadows ready to pounce. We live in our heads. Maybe my mother knew that too. I suspect that she did.

I did the usual teenage things as that second year passed, drifting inevitably into the third. I drank too much alcohol and experimented with illicit drugs, one mind-numbing chemical hit after another, but if anything my experimentation made things worse. The nightmares intensified, the flashbacks became more vivid, restful sleep was beyond my reach as the darkness stretched out until dawn's welcome light crept over the distant horizon. I was always on high alert, tense, stressed; however well things seemed to be going in the world outside my mind. And sleep was difficult, I woke often and still do. I've since realised that I was suffering post-traumatic stress, like that suffered by combat veterans. It's not something that's ever been formally diagnosed but I've got no doubts it's the case. An unwelcome legacy of my father's vile attentions that I still endure. But I got on with life as best I could. I'm still proud of that, one day at a time, trying to look forward rather than back, clinging onto the hope of better times ahead.

I won, I won, I won, the bastard's gone.

I repeated it often, almost believing it, but not quite. He was always there, you see, somewhere in the background. A gradually fading dark shadow of his former self, but still only too real to me. I think of him less often now. But he still visits from time to time, in my weaker moments, when something reminds me of the past. His memory seems indestructible. He still haunts me however many times I kill in his name. He even talks to me sometimes, mocking, undermining my confidence, whispering in my ear. I fear he always will.

I qualified at the age of twenty-one. I passed, me, I was one of the educated classes. Let's focus on the positives for once. And then, only weeks later, I got the job that would cement my future. I was to be an admin officer with the local probation service. I won't say where. I've probably said too much already, offered too many clues. But please don't assume a part of me wants to be caught. Arrest is the last thing I want. I can't avoid the telling. That job was truly pivotal. It gave me virtually unrestricted access to information, access to files.

And I learnt something terrible, something that blew my world apart when I first began my new role. I wasn't the only one who'd suffered the vile attentions of a predator. There are other monsters out there. Monster men like my father. Some *even worse* than my father. And any number of survivors, people like me who hold no blame and did nothing to deserve their fate. I read the details of one case after another, incredulous as to the harm such hunters of innocence chose to inflict on their many victims. I knew then that I had to do something, something positive, something proactive. It became an obsession. Nothing else mattered. It was as if a bulb had switched on in my head. For the first time ever, my true purpose was clear. I was to turn the tables. The hunted was to become the hunter.

I bided my time, researched, gathered information, and planned until I thought the time was exactly right to act. I like to think of myself as a crusader, a purveyor of righteous justice, a force for good in a dark and foreboding world of woe. But not everyone is going to see it that way. People get offended by the slightest thing these days. We're members of a snowflake generation. You only need to look at social media to know that.

But please remember this before you jump to any ready conclusions. There's any number of predators still out there, in your town, maybe even in your neighbourhood. Men like my father. Men who target the innocent. Monsters who can spot the vulnerable in the blink of an eye.

I'm comfortable with the decisions I've made. And I've still got work to do. It's far from over. I'll have more blood on my hands before this story ends. I'm trying to hold back the tide.

9

Two years have now passed since my college graduation. I've got the framed certificate on my lounge wall. I still work for the probation service in the same administrative role. But the bedsit of my youth is a mere memory. I live in a two-bedroom detached cottage these days. It's remote, deep in the countryside with no near neighbours. It was somewhat in need of updating when I first bought it, with my mother's generous help, one last financial gesture to compensate for the unspoken past. But I've done the place up since, as best I can, one room at a time, counting the pennies as I went. It's far from luxurious even after all my efforts. But it's practical, exactly what I need, and that's what matters.

My cottage is surrounded by mature trees and high hedges, down a country lane away from inquisitive eyes. A small house with a useful outbuilding, once a pigsty, but now serving a very different purpose in the warmer months, that I'll come to in good time.

The place is a bit of a drive from town, five miles from the main road and then on from there. But that's not a bad thing, the distance has its advantages, as I'm sure you'll come to appreciate. The location offers secrecy when needed; that's why I chose it in the first place. There are no overlooking houses, and no curtain-twitchers sticking their noses in where they don't belong. And that suits me just fine. I couldn't function otherwise.

I was sitting in my small cottage kitchen not so very long ago, a short time before writing these words, with my recently acquired, state-of-the-art laptop resting, open and fully charged, on the pine table in front of me. That's usually how I work these days, next to the radiator, close to the kettle. Keeping warm matters in the winter months. There's a dusting of snow on the fields. I could see it through the kitchen window until the light faded. A chocolate box blanket of white that's pleasing to the eye. It makes digging the ground more difficult, of course, that's always a concern when the temperature drops. But there's always an answer to a problem if you think about it for long enough. There's more than one way to dispose of a body. You just have to use your imagination.

I sit on an old wooden stool rather than using a cushion. I don't like to be too comfortable when I'm working. A bit of discomfort gives me an edge. I need to stay focused, on top of my game. I positioned myself on the very edge of my stool, staring at the laptop screen and tapping the computer keys, not nearly as quickly as I'd have liked. I've tried to develop my typing skills, to speed things up, to operate more efficiently. But that skill still seems beyond me despite so much practise, and so I accept my limitations.

I wear a pair of those blue-light blocking plastic glasses as I work, perched on the tip of my nose. Can you picture the scene? I feel sure you can. It's a simple enough scenario, me, the kitchen, my computer.

I'll move on to tell you more once I've calmed myself down a bit. Some of the things I see on the screen get my blood boiling. I feel such a sense of responsibility for the safety of children. I sometimes wish I could look away and ignore the horrors I encounter online. But it's not in my nature to turn a blind eye. If only I could! My world would be a simpler place.

I was posing as a ten-year-old schoolgirl in an online chat room about an hour ago. That's what I do, I create a character, like an actor, sometimes a boy and sometimes a girl, whichever works best with my particular target in mind. Now, do you get the picture? I was the bait, the lure, searching for perverts, drawing them in. And tonight, right there on the computer screen, there was a predator that caught my interest immediately.

I'd been looking out for him for some time now, not for weeks but months, and then there he was. He's in his late forties, an ex-primary school teacher, a father and grandfather, on probation having avoided prison, as the bastards sometimes do. He'd been caught with thousands of indecent images of children, many in the worst category, including torture. It doesn't get any more dangerous than that. I'd read all about him at work. It's all there in the files, readily available information, just what I need to make my plans.

I'd expressed concern in the office months before, with feeling, talking to his probation officer over a coffee in the staffroom one lunchtime. I said I thought the man was a high-risk offender. I even explained why. That his interests were extreme. That his offending had escalated over time, and would again.

Those vile photographs he's so very fond of told their own awful story. They aren't just digital images; they're real living and breathing children, every single one of them. Children experiencing unspeakable horrors, as I did. I tried to explain all that, to elucidate my concerns. But my words of caution fell on predictably deaf ears.

I'm not qualified, you see. I'm just an admin officer, and so it seems my opinion doesn't count for much, if at all. I suspected this particular offender would go on to re-offend. And I couldn't have been more right. Tonight, there he was again, on my laptop screen, trawling for victims, predatory, menacing, the worst kind of man. Monsters like him don't change. They are what they are. They do what they do. It's why I do what I do. My deeds are my obsession, as my target's crimes are theirs.

This particular sex offender calls himself Big Boy! It would be funny if it weren't so pathetic. I knew exactly who he was as soon as I saw that name on my computer screen. The shit-stain is so full of himself, so seemingly self-confident as he plies his filthy trade. My anger is rising again now as I recall his messages. Vile words sent without conscience or care. How dare he send such abominations to a person he thought a child? What's wrong with the man? He's broken, something's missing.

If I don't stop him, then who will? I could report him to the authorities, of course, I could pass on the evidence I've gleaned. But what would that achieve? He may go to prison for a few months at best, and then he'd be out again, destroying more lives, robbing other children of their childhoods, doing his thing. That's not good enough, it's not nearly good enough, not in my world, not while I can still draw breath.

I actually thought that Big Boy might have ended our online conversation at one point. That he'd wriggled off the hook, slithering back under the nearest stone. The slimeball stopped typing for a time, but he soon began again. And then he told me everything I needed to know. He was a lover of children. That's what the bastard claimed. A lover! A fucking lover! That's one word for it. An abuser would be a better one. It was more of the same. It's always the same.

He wanted to get to know me better, to meet up, to be my special friend. And then he sent photos. Of course, he did. It doesn't take much imagination to guess of what. First came a picture of his flabby milk-white body, from the neck down, of course. Monster men like Big Boy never reveal their faces. And then a second image focused on his genitals. He was erect. They almost always are. Gross! No surprises there. It made me feel physically sick. I dry gagged, once, then again.

He was nothing if not predictable. Always manipulative, always with his deviant goals in mind. That's why the predatory monster was online all along. That was why he trawled the internet in search of the vulnerable. And now he thought he'd found his next victim. How very wrong could a monster be? If I played my cards right, I'd have him. My trap was set. Now all I had to do was play him, to reel him in.

Did you like my photos?

Like them? *Fucking well like them!* The *bastard*, the total and utter *bastard*! I spat tiny globules of warm saliva at the screen, my face contorting with rage. I replied that I did. I liked them very much. I responded in childlike language, my online message including deliberate grammatical errors that wouldn't ring alarm bells in the monster's head. I wrote as I imagine a ten-year-old does. It's something I've practised. And it worked well, as I expected it would. Big Boy asked me to reciprocate, to send photos of my own, naked photos, a ten-year-old schoolgirl, or so he thought. But that was never going to happen. I typed *maybe next time* and waited. Tap away; you slug, you rat, you monster, you curse on all that's good.

I waited, resisting the temptation to start typing again, giving the bastard time to sign his death warrant. That's how these things work. And Big Boy was no different, which didn't surprise me in the slightest.

I was relieved that my new target obviously hadn't suspected a thing when he finally began typing again minutes later. He was telling me what he'd like to do to me now, in ghastly graphic detail. He was telling me what he'd like me to do to him. He really was a repulsive creature, one of the worst I've encountered. I replied that his deviant wants sounded like fun. Without using those words, of course. I added that I'd seen sex films online. Videos of things I'd like to do myself when given a chance. The slug suggested meeting up at that point, and I knew I had him. What an utterly revolting man!

So, you'll meet me? We can have some fun together, like the grown-ups you saw in the videos?

I replied that I was so up for it and that we could do *everything* he wanted. And then I waited for him to start typing again, as I knew he inevitably would.

We could make our own film. That would be fun. I could bring a camera when we meet. You could be a star.

I said that it all sounded so very exciting. Just what the pervert wanted to read. Anything to lure him in.

And then he promised presents, anything I wanted if I satisfied his needs. If I'd be his special friend.

I said I wanted a new smartphone, to which he readily agreed. He was playing his best cards now. He really believed he was in control. He'd give me anything I wanted, as long as I told no one. As long as it remained our secret.

Where do you live?

Ah! That was his next move. He was upping the ante. I laughed when he asked that. A cold laugh that had nothing to do with humour. That was *precisely* the question I'd been waiting for. I told him exactly where I live. I wanted him to know. I *needed* him to know. That's the way I deal with these things – face to face, up close and personal.

Okay, that's good, I know the area, you're only about an hour's drive from where I live. Do you think we could meet up somewhere nearby? I could take you somewhere really nice in my new car. Somewhere we could be alone to have some fun together. And I'll bring the phone. That's a promise! You do want the phone, don't you?

What makes scum like Big Boy think their behaviour is even remotely acceptable? Can anyone answer that for me? How do slugs like him live with themselves? How do they sleep nights? Some claim they like children too much. Even that they do no harm. Are they really that deluded? Or are they simply too focused on their own perverted wants to worry about anyone else. I think that's probably it. It's the only thing that makes any sense to me. Men like Big Boy, men like my father, understand the damage they do. They just don't care.

I waited for a minute or two before responding to his latest question, upping his anticipation. I took a slow, deep breath, watching the seconds tick by on the wall clock above the chest freezer to my right. Then I wrote the words I knew he'd be delighted to read: Yes, I wanted the phone. And I'd love to meet him too. It all sounded like a fun time.

And that was when I truly drove home my advantage. I typed quickly, using two fingers, the best I could do despite my years of study. I told him that my parents would be away for the day the following Sunday. I then added that I'm an only child. I'm sure he loved that. And finally that I'd be home alone, bored, keen for entertainment, and I didn't have any neighbours. So, why not meet at my home address?

Those weren't my exact words. I dumbed it down for the pervert's ready consumption. I was sure not to scare him off with my intelligence or maturity. Raising alarm bells is the last thing I'd have wanted. So I was careful, as I always am. My methods had worked before, and I had no reason to think they wouldn't again. He was probably thinking along the same lines, but for very different reasons.

What colour phone do you want?

I typed, *Pink, I love pink.*

Ah, okay, pink makes the girls wink, pink it is. Anything your little heart desires. Are you certain your parents will be away all day? You really need to be sure. That's REALLY important!

I replied that I was sure, something I'm confident he was desperate to confirm. I bet he couldn't believe his luck. I pictured him drooling, wanking as if his worthless life depended on it. And I'd never hated a monster man more.

I typed my address, told him we'd be safe, that we wouldn't be caught.

What time shall I come?

Ha! The misguided fool. He really thought he was winning. But of course, he was wrong. Horribly, irrevocably wrong. If he thought he was grooming me, he was very sadly mistaken. The predator had become quarry. Just like my father, as he walked along that cliff path all those years ago. Oh yes, this sick bastard would pay too, as Father had. Not in the same way, of course, but the outcome would be much the same. Big Boy would meet me; he'd come to my home, deep in the Welsh countryside, where no one else can see. I'd look him right in the eye, our noses almost touching. He'd get to know me so very well. But he wouldn't enjoy the experience nearly as much as he hoped.

10

Preparing for a new guest's arrival is always a complex business. Big Boy will be my third caller in a matter of months, so I'm getting better at the process, learning from mistakes, building on what went well. Everything has to be just right for things to go smoothly. I've got just over twenty-four hours before he comes knocking on my door. That should be more than enough time to get everything in place, and more than enough time to worry.

What if he doesn't turn up? That's my main concern; I'd hate him to slither away at this late stage. But I don't think that's very likely. Slugs like Big Boy live for times like this when they anticipate indulging their aberrant needs, feeding their fantasies, making them real. He'll be counting down the minutes, counting the seconds, such things define him. And I use that fact to my advantage. I like to think of myself as a purveyor of righteous justice, a force for good, jury, judge and executioner. I'll tear him apart, rip him to pieces once convicted. His life will end in a dark world of pain. But please don't feel sorry for him. The monster deserves no less. He has no idea of the storm coming his way.

And so I'll continue to prepare as the hours pass. Everything has to be all set, everything in its place, ready for any eventuality; there's no room for errors. He looks flabby but strong in the photos. He's a big man, at least six feet and two inches tall, and heavy, very heavy. I'm only a little over nine stone in weight myself. That always has to be a consideration. It's some contrast, Mr Big and Miss Little. There are limits to my physical prowess. I'll have to use my intellect and cunning to defeat him with my mind. I have to be cleverer than he is, which shouldn't be difficult. He'll only be focused on one thing. He'll be thinking with his dick.

The clear plastic sheeting is ready. A big roll of it was brought to my door by a delivery man in a large white van with a bright blue logo on the side. I don't know what it said, but it hardly matters. He seemed like a pleasant enough guy on first impressions. However, you can never really tell. Be careful whom you trust; that's my advice. Monsters come in many forms.

I wondered if the delivery man asked himself what I wanted with all that plastic. Or if he'd worked out the kind of woman I am. Could he see the killer instinct in my eyes? It concerned me for a time. But I really don't think he could. I was probably worrying about nothing. I remember him smiling as he helped me get the heavy roll into the cottage hall. I didn't let him into my killing room for obvious reasons. That space is reserved exclusively for guests. In the end, he drove away without comment. As if nothing untoward was happening.

I think there's plenty of plastic sheeting left for Big Boy plus whoever comes next. I've got a couple of likely candidates on my shortlist, monster men in need of stopping when the time is right. But my list may change depending on the assessed risk posed by individual offenders. I try to be as flexible as possible as new information comes to light. I find that works best for me.

It's how I maximise my impact. There's any number of sex offenders out there – more than you could ever imagine. I can't kill all of them, however much I'd like to. It's a matter of priorities.

My doctor recently prescribed me a two-week supply of sleeping medication. She does that from time to time when I can be sufficiently persuasive. I cry, lower my gaze, play the needy patient, and she grabs her prescription pad with eager fingers, glad to get me out of there as quickly as possible. The medication is a green, sticky liquid in a clear plastic bottle with a black screw top, instead of tablets. The liquid may well come in useful. I'll use it if I have to, to pour down Big Boy's throat, to sedate him, to take away his strength. But only if it's essential. Only if all else fails to subdue him. There's a limited supply after all. I may need to use it for somebody else.

I've prepared my various butcher's tools and knives, laying them out in order of size, next to a hammer I always keep handy. There's a filleting knife with a ten-inch blade that's a particular favourite; a utility knife with a short, strong replaceable blade that's great for slicing; an old Scottish dagger with a bone handle, bought cheaply at auction, that's ideal for stabbing one body part or another as the need arises; a bone saw; and finally a cleaver. All are practical, and all are useful. They've been thoroughly cleaned, polished and sharpened. There's no room for sloppiness. If you're going to do something, why not do it properly? That's the way I look at it. I take pride in my work.

I'll use one or all of the implements, depending on how things go. Big Boy's end may be quick, or it may be slow. I have no way of knowing before I meet him. That really does depend on what he says, how he responds to my questions and observations, that's down to him. I can't take responsibility for the actions of others. But either way, he'll pay an appropriate price for his crimes. That's a done deal. He's as guilty as sin. Yes, he'll pay, it's just a matter of how.

I use a room off the hall as my killing room in the winter months. I like to work in relative comfort whenever I can. I call the room my slaughterhouse. It's a space I only use for one purpose. An empty room with no furniture or carpet, just bare floorboards that I cover in my plastic sheeting, secured by strong yellow tape I buy in a local hardware store, several rolls at a time. The walls are painted with a good quality white washable paint, of the type used in bathrooms. That's of crucial importance when cleaning up. Although I can still see bloodstains in a few places I've missed or didn't wash down sufficiently well if I look hard enough with my contact lenses in. I keep the thick red velvet curtains shut to keep out the daylight in the interests of privacy. But that's not a problem; there's a bright ceiling light at the centre of the room, just a bulb, no lampshade. I need to see what I'm doing as the process progresses. And there's a small stainless-steel sink, the one little luxury I've allowed myself, installed by an acquaintance of my mother, a man she met in church. She still goes, can you believe that, after everything that happened? Each to their own, I guess, her attendance does no harm that I can think of. But it's certainly not for me.

I think I've told you more than enough for now. I've set the scene. I've given you an idea of what to expect next. I won't continue my story again until after Big Boy's been and the deed is done. I need to concentrate on my primary purpose. My diary has to come second.

Oh, there is one last thing I wanted to mention before bringing this session to a timely close. I've discovered that I can dictate directly to my new laptop. I no longer need to write anything down, and that's an undoubted bonus given my typing skills, or rather the lack of them. I should be able to speed up my tale-telling from this point in, once I'm washed and sufficiently rested. Entertaining a guest is exhausting, dirty work. I know that from hard-won experience. It's amazing how much blood one body can hold. There are pints of the stuff, flowing red, it gets everywhere.

The next chapter is likely to be somewhat gory if you're of a sensitive disposition. It may be challenging to read for some. But try to remember who I'm killing. Remind yourself who I'm chopping up for safe disposal. That may help you cope a little better. It certainly does me.

11

The minutes before a guest finally arrives are the worst for me. They seem to drag on forever, eating away at my sanity, clawing at my peace of mind. And this time was no different. Big Boy was a few minutes late. The *bastard*, the total and utter *bastard*! For one horrible moment, I thought the scumbag wasn't coming at all. That he'd bottled out or seen through my trickery. I stared through my bedroom window, watching the lane leading to the cottage, willing his car to appear. I felt my gut twist as I checked my watch for the third time in a matter of minutes, my head starting to ache as my legs weakened, threatening to collapse under me with the stress of it all. But then there he was in front of me, driving slowly down the lane in a dirty blue saloon car, the make of which I couldn't identify. He was on his way, that's what counted. He was about to enter my world. The time had come. All my preparations had led to this.

I continued watching, dropping to my knees, crouching, hidden, as the monster in human form parked his car in the yard outside the cottage. I could see him staring through his windscreen, his neck craned, his nose almost touching the glass.

He was studying the building with quick darting eyes, from right to left, up, down and back again, as if he was trying to look through the windows, even the impenetrable stone walls, to weigh up the risks, to figure out his next move.

I feared that the monster man might lose his nerve at any second, and drive away, to escape me when I was so very close to success. But no, my concerns were unjustified. He exited the car, closing the driver's door behind him, placing his car keys in a trouser pocket with chubby, sausage fingers that made me laugh despite the tension. I'd parked my car well out of sight, to avoid alarming him, and that was a good thing, a wise precautionary move. He was walking slowly, looking around him as he approached my front door, glancing in every direction, even behind him, more than once, his head moving in quick, sharp, sudden movements.

I rushed downstairs as he knocked on the door, reticently at first, his knock barely audible even in the silence. Then, louder and more insistent as I entered my slaughterhouse, dressed only in disposable white paper overalls, ready, using a computer-generated voice to call out to him from inside a hidden recess in the wall that couldn't be seen from the hall. The laptop mimicked a childlike female voice I'd developed and perfected over time. I pressed a key to start the process.

'Come in; the door's not locked. I'm in here. I'm waiting for you.'

He must have realised I'd left the front door slightly ajar by that time. He could push the door open if he chose to. Nothing was stopping him entering the building other than his reticence. But he didn't open it, or at least not yet. I had to draw him in. I had to tempt him still further. I used my computer to lure him again, choosing one of several available pre-recorded options, as the door opened just far enough for him to place his bulbous, balding head through the resulting gap. He was listening intently, his head tilted at a slight angle, considering his next step.

'Come on in. What are you waiting for? We can have some fun together. It's open, the door's open, come on in.'

I waited, watching, willing him to enter. *Come on, monster, in you come, in you come. My slaughterhouse is awaiting you.*

And then as I silently repeated my mantra, he pushed my front door fully open. I heard the familiar creak as the door swung on its hinges, and resisted my inclination to cheer as he stepped over the doorstep entering my domain. He was standing just inside the hall now, the door still open behind him, a fly in my web, a rat in my trap. He didn't know it yet, but I was in control.

Come on, Big Boy, come on, monster man, in you come, in you come.

I repeated it in my head, willing it to become a reality. I was still carefully hidden, clutching the knife in my left hand so very tightly that my fingers ached. And then, as he took a forward step, I heard his voice for the very first time. Big Boy emitted a high-pitched sound, seemingly so unsuited to a man of his height and fleshy build. He had an English accent too, which surprised me. Southern maybe, I can't be sure, but certainly not the Welsh lilt I'd expected. I peered out from the concealed alcove as he walked on down the hall for a second or two, ever so slowly, ever so cautiously, before stopping again. Even then, I could see him shaking as he stood there, shifting his not inconsiderable weight from one foot to another, his involuntary dance revealing his nervous state.

The monster's words were hissed, almost whispered, but still audible to my sensitive ears, as I waited my opportunity to strike.

'Where are you?'

I pressed play, my computer replying in that same girlish voice, telling him exactly what he wanted to hear. He was so close to acting out his fantasies. Or, so he thought. He could smell it, taste it, almost touch it – this middle-aged man who preyed on the innocent.

'I'm in here, I'm waiting for you, in the room at the end of the hall.'

'I've, er, I've got the phone for you, it's a pink one, just like you asked for. Show yourself.'

'I'm shy. I'm nervous. I've never done anything like this before. You have to come to me.'

I think he almost turned and ran at that point. I could see it in his eyes. I could spot the tension in his face. He looked so close to panic as if the unusual circumstances raised questions that he couldn't silence. But there was a prominent bulge in the monster man's trousers that I couldn't fail to see as he peered into the semi-darkness, seeing a childlike mannequin I'd placed in a far corner, seated on the floor. His hormones drove him on, his perverted desires at the forefront of his mind, overwhelming his misgivings. There was no running, no retreat. He slowly approached my slaughterhouse one step at a time.

'Are you alone?'

'Yes, there's just me.'

He was at the door to the room now, sweating, the stink of his body odour filling my nostrils as he peered into the semi-darkness.

'Have your parents definitely left? There's no one else in the house but you and me?'

'Yes, they won't be back for ages.'

His eyes narrowed. 'Why are you in the dark?'

I responded this time, rather than use the laptop. I didn't have a suitable pre-prepared choice of words. I giggled, trying to sound shy, bashful. I think he liked that.

He seemed persuaded to me. And that was it. It was all the temptation he needed. One second he was safe, standing out of my reach in the hall, and then he was in my slaughterhouse, standing there, blinking as his eyes adapted to the gloom. I knew the time to act had come as he walked slowly towards the curtains a few seconds later, reaching out to open them to let in the light.

I crept out from my hiding place, leaping forwards with practised ability and speed, the razor-sharp knife raised high above my head in a frenzy of co-ordinated activity.

He turned to face me just as I brought the knife crashing down, using all my strength and weight to sink the steel blade deep into his upper chest, the tip hitting bone and almost jarring the weapon from my hand. I screamed in delight as he staggered backwards, bouncing off the wall behind him, sinking to the plastic-covered floor like a slowly deflating blow-up toy.

I left him lying there, incredulous and groaning, as I flicked a switch on the wall to my left, flooding the room with a bright white light that made us both squint. For one terrible moment, I thought I might have killed him prematurely, as I saw bubbles of blood and saliva erupting from his open mouth. But there was still the spark of life in those red eyes of his. He wasn't ready to die quite yet. I've never seen a man so confused, so bewildered or fearful. It brought a smile to my face as he spoke.

'What, what, who... w-why?'

'Silence!' I shouted it three times before he finally shut up.

'This is the court of your victims, Big Boy. You were convicted in your absence. It's time to pay the price of your sins. Have you anything to say for yourself in mitigation before I issue your death warrant?'

His voice was quieter now, slightly garbled as he struggled onto his side, spitting out a mouthful of blood, forcing out his words. 'I'm– I'm not a p-paedo. I hate those dirty bastards. I'd n-never hurt a child.'

What utter shit. Was that really the best he could do? 'Then, why are you here?'

'I c-came to the wrong address.' Big Boy still had the strength to talk, which pleased me. But his words had angered me even further. He was so full of crap. It spewed from his mouth in a torrent of lies. If he'd taken responsibility for his crimes, I would at least have respected him for that. But his filthy denial was no more than I'd expected. He had no redeeming features. Or, at least, none I could identify. Even now, he was trying to hide his true nature.

I knelt at the monster's side, the blood-stained knife still in my hand. 'Don't waste what little's left of your breath. I know *exactly* what you are, Big Boy, or should I call you Gavin, Gavin Michael Taylor. That's your name, isn't it? I've read your probation file, every single word of it. I know *all* about your interests, your collection of photos, those awful pictures portraying so much pain and distress. And now it's your turn to suffer. There's a price to pay for your actions. Think of it as karma. Have you got anything to say for yourself before it's too late?'

He didn't respond to my allegations, not directly. I already knew he had no intention of confessing. So what on earth could he have said? I knew his time was fast running out as he pleaded for his life, asking for help, an ambulance, talking of his children, his wife. He was trying to seem human. But he was wasting his breath. His family would be better off without him. He was a monster to me, and no more than that.

I did consider torturing Big Boy before death. I'd thought of inflicting similar abominations to which some of the poor children in those vile photos had been subjected. The ones that turned him on so very much, feeding his fantasies. But that sad excuse for a man seemed so utterly pathetic as he lost control of his bowels. So unworthy of my continued attention as he pissed himself while choking on his blood. I couldn't stand to interact with that waste of breath even for a second longer than I had to. Just being in his presence made me feel dirty. I wanted him dead. I wanted him butchered, and his body out of there; one less predator in the world of the living.

'Do you have any last words before I bring your miserable life to an end?'

'No, p-please, I'm– I'm s-sorry, please, I... I–'

'Shut the fuck up! Stop your fucking whimpering. It won't do you any favours. I've never heard anything as pathetic in my life.'

But he didn't shut up. His pleading intensified. I'd heard more than enough. There was only one way to silence him. I raised myself on my knees, looming over him, speaking loudly, insistently, not allowing him to finish his pitiful, snivelling pleadings. 'Now would be a good time to seek forgiveness from your maker, if you believe in such things.'

And he did start praying as I raised the blade high above my head, clutching the slippery wet shaft with both hands, raining down blow after bloody blow until all was silence. And that was it; the deed was done. Big Boy was no longer a threat to me or anybody else.

I rose to my feet, filthy and panting, as Big Boy's body fluids pooled around his corpse, flooding the floor with filth. I looked around me, yawning as the adrenalin in my system gradually subsided. The killing had been exhausting. I felt so very tired, as exhausted as I've ever been in my life. As I searched the monster's trouser pockets for his car keys, I acknowledged I needed sustenance, I needed rest, to be at my best, to avoid mistakes. I'd have to get rid of his car, of course, later that night, to somewhere safe, somewhere I wouldn't be implicated. But for now, I'd hide it behind the cottage, next to mine, where it wouldn't be seen by any delivery drivers or other unexpected callers. That couldn't be delayed even for a second longer. The risks were too high for that. But I was tired now, weary. I had a change of heart. Big Boy could stay where he was until the following day. What was the rush? I could take my time. The monster man could keep me company. A night as my guest wouldn't do any harm at all.

I turned slowly away, walking down the hall towards the front door, satisfied with my rumination, feeling rather full of myself, my ego boosted. I'd done well, really well. Now all I had to do was keep it up, one job at a time. Bite-sized chunks and I'll be fine.

12

I set my alarm clock for 3am on Sunday morning, a perfect time for subterfuge when most of the population are asleep and lost to their dreams. I threw back my winter weight quilt, jumped from bed with forced enthusiasm, and opened the bedroom curtains, looking out on a winter wonderland that raised my flagging spirits despite the early hour. I can still appreciate beauty from time to time in my ugly world of woe. It doesn't happen often, but it does happen. And this was one of those rare moments as a bright three-quarter moon illuminated the snow-covered countryside in every direction.

The world can be such a wondrous place if one ignores the horrors. If I'd grown up in a very different family, who knows where my life would have taken me? Maybe I could have enjoyed more moments like that. Perhaps then I wouldn't have a human slaughterhouse splashed red with blood.

I dressed in my warmest clothing, incorporating several natural fibre layers, topped with a thick, warm woollen jumper bought in a second-hand shop several weeks before. I made a quick bathroom visit before heading downstairs, full of good intentions despite my inevitable fatigue. I'd given some thought to the safe disposal of the monster man's car before finally drifting off to sleep. Options were limited, but I was confident of success if I remained vigilant and stuck to a plan. I've found that staying positive is crucial to my holding things together. I can't let practicalities get me down.

I'd finally settled on a nearby beach as a good disposal point. It seemed ideal with several miles of flat, hard sand and a fast-rising tide, which wouldn't be full in until 3.55am. I intended to drive down a conveniently located concrete ramp used by my family in times gone by, park the car at the tideline, abandoning the vehicle to the rising sea. I felt sure that the saltwater would more than adequately destroy any evidence of my involvement, fingerprints, fibres, DNA and the like. Planning is everything given my vocation. I can't protect the innocent if I'm locked up in a cell. I'm a dark-clad executioner in a good cause. That amused me when I thought of it in those terms. It's the classic case of two wrongs making a right.

I glanced in at Big Boy's lifeless body as I passed my slaughterhouse door on my way to the kitchen. His corpse was stiffening by then, and his blood coagulated. He had a look of shock on his face. As if, even in death, he couldn't quite believe the price he'd paid for his sins. The scene gave me a warm sense of accomplishment as I yawned and rubbed my eyes.

A quick, strong cup of coffee sweetened with a little coconut sugar, and I was ready to go. I pulled on a warm coat, clutched Big Boy's car keys, sprayed generous amounts of lavender air freshener in every first-floor room to mask the invasive smell of excrement in preparation for my return, and made my way outside, locking the front door behind me as I went. I sucked in long deep breaths of cold night-time air, filling my lungs as I made my way to the rear of the cottage, coat fastened, collar up, and a woolly hat pulled low over my head. I thought the hat an inspired idea, one of my best. I'd adjusted it carefully, hiding my short brown hair. And I was wearing bright red plastic rimmed glasses, rather than my usual contact lenses. Not the world's most imaginative disguise, but a disguise nonetheless. I'd use the back roads and avoid any cameras, but I didn't want to be recognised in the unlikely event I was seen. I think my outfit achieved that aim pretty damned well. As I've said before, getting caught was never a part of the plan.

I unlocked and started Big Boy's car without any problems at all, but it was a manual gear shift, in contrast to my automatic, which caused me some concern. I punched the steering wheel hard and felt slightly better almost immediately. My initial rage was subsiding as my breathing slowed. Driving the car was one more obstacle to overcome and no more than that.

I stalled the unfamiliar vehicle's engine three times as I manoeuvred to the front of the cottage in first gear. That disappointed me. I don't appreciate failure. I see it as a weakness, something I can't allow myself to indulge. It's too risky in my world, too dangerous. It threatens my freedom. I feared spiralling into a cycle of despair as my world became a darker and more forbidding place. But by the time I drove up my lane towards the country road, I felt back in control only minutes later. I'd owned a manual geared car in the past, and the old motor skills were fast returning. I wouldn't go as far as to say I liked driving the car. That would be something of an exaggeration. But it was something I could cope with. My feelings of failure abated almost as quickly as they'd arisen. I reminded myself that there was one less predator in the world because of me. Any amount of effort on my part was worth it to achieve that goal. I'd done a good thing, a worthy thing; I told myself that I shouldn't be too hard on myself. And I'd dealt with a lot worse.

It took me a little over half an hour to reach my destination of choice. I was in a more positive mood by that point, singing along to the radio as I went. That same concrete ramp I'd remembered from my troubled childhood was still there when I reached the seaside village, leading directly onto a beach once used for world land speed record attempts in glory days gone by. I glanced around me, both pleased and relieved to see no potential witnesses as I drove slowly down the gradual incline onto the firm sand. The clear moonlit sky had clouded over by then, with a flurry of snowflakes seemingly coming from every direction at once. As if God was mocking me, laughing at my plans. But I focused with a new-found determination. I was there for a reason. I had to get on with it.

I switched the car's headlights to the main beam on the second hurried attempt, increased the speed of the wipers, and headed towards the sea, about 100 metres away. When I reached the tideline, I could see that the water was rising quickly, making its way over the fresh sand at a reasonably fast walking pace. I felt elated. My plan was coming together exactly as I'd hoped. My spirits leapt and danced as I engaged first gear. I pressed my foot down hard on the accelerator pedal and entered the water. All was good at first. But the car came to a sputtering halt when the seawater reached the halfway point of the front wheels. I forced the driver's door open, which was more difficult than I'd imagined, enabling me to step out into the sea, the freezing temperature of which made me gasp. I almost stumbled and fell at the water's edge, but I regained my balance with quick-moving feet that were already numb with cold. What the hell was I thinking?

Stupid girl!

I could hear my father's critical voice chastising me as he had so often in life.

You ridiculous girl!

I resented his mocking words but he had a point. I shouldn't have got wet. I should have left the car parked at the tideline as I'd originally planned. The sea would have taken care of the rest.

My father's voice continued to echo in my ears as I made my way back up the beach towards the ramp. He scolded me repeatedly, jeering, sneering, lowering my mood. But as I reached the ramp, looking back at the car, which was slowly disappearing under the waves, I drove the self-serving bastard from my mind. My plan had worked exactly as I'd envisaged. There were no witnesses. Or, at least, none of which I was aware. And all viable evidence would be destroyed. I was confident of that. No one could link me to the car or its recently deceased owner. That was a triumph in my eyes. I had to stay hopeful and focus on the positives. The night wasn't over. It was going to be a long walk home.

13

I've thought long and hard as to whether to share this part of my story with you at all. It won't be easy for some to read. It certainly wasn't easy for me to write. I want you to know that.

Please be under no misapprehension. I'm not one of life's ghouls. I don't enjoy the company of corpses, their unquestioning compliance to my every whim and desire. The way the dead look, smell and feel. It's a case of necessity for me rather than pleasure.

I can't push every monster off a cliff. I only wish I could. If I kill a monster man, I have to get rid of the body. I'm sure you'll agree that's reasonable. I can't leave the corpse lying around my house to rot for weeks on end. I tried it once for a week or two when I killed my first guest. I couldn't face cutting him up. I couldn't figure out what to do with the corpse. Decay sets in, then maggots, then insects. The flesh breaks down, it blackens, and the smell becomes intolerable even to me. And so quick disposal is a necessity rather than a luxury – something I've had to learn to do within a reasonable time of death. It's surprising what one can get used to.

I rang in sick early on Monday morning, claiming a stomach

upset when I spoke to my boss. It's not something I'm proud of doing. I like to think of myself as a conscientious employee. I value my integrity. But my trek home from the beach was totally exhausting. I was in one hell of a state by the time I reached my door. You should have seen the condition of my feet. I stripped off my sodden clothes, showered, set my alarm, and then fell into bed to adequately rest. I was going to need all the energy I could muster. Dismembering a corpse can be a surprisingly demanding process, even with the right tools and my degree of experience. Cutting through the flesh is easy enough if a blade is sharp. I guess that's obvious to anyone who thinks about it. But sawing through bones can be onerous. You may not realise that in your very different world. It surprised me too the first time I had to do it. And the mess, I couldn't believe the mess. Thank goodness for the plastic sheeting. The body fluids get everywhere. Cleaning up is a job in itself.

I went back to bed for a couple of hours after contacting my boss. Big Boy was a large man. I needed to be at my best. I got up for a second time at a little after eleven. I made myself some breakfast, just a bowl of cereal, turned up the heating, and then stripped off completely. Cutting up a body leaves one covered in blood. There's no avoiding it however hard one tries. It gets everywhere, and I do mean *everywhere*, into every nook and crevice, even in my hair and ears. I like to shower straight away afterwards. I make sure the water's piping hot, use plenty of scented soap, and keep scrubbing for as long as it takes. I like to be clean.

I collected my butchers' equipment together at about 11.30am, laying the tools out on the plastic-covered floor for convenience before making a start. I like to work to the sound of favourite CDs, turning the music up loud, so it fills the room. I work to a rhythm, cutting, sawing, and singing along, occasionally standing up and dancing when the mood takes me.

I hope that doesn't make me sound callous. That's the last thing I'd want. As I've said, the dissection process is a demanding task. It can become tedious, unpleasant even, at times. The music helps with that. It lightens my mood.

It took me almost two hours to dismember Big Boy to my satisfaction. I removed his big old head first, rolling it aside before moving on to the arms and legs. He was big-boned, so removing each limb took some considerable time and effort even with my sharpest bone saw. And my God, he was heavy. Every limb was hard to lift as I wrapped it in black plastic bin bags for later disposal. Even the arms made me stagger, let alone the legs.

I was truly flagging by the time I finished, lying naked and panting next to the monster man's torso. I lay there resting, breathing slowly, in through my nose and out through my mouth, gradually regaining my strength. I hadn't enjoyed the process. I want to stress that. I can't say it enough. I was glad to get it over with. Bagging the final limb was a relief. But there was a sense of achievement too, of a job well done. I think that's fair to say. But it wasn't over.

Now I had to get rid of the body parts. I had some ideas. The ground was still frozen, so burial wasn't an option. I had to come up with a viable alternative. I did consider leaving the bagged body parts outside in the pigsty for however long it took until the inevitable thaw. It seemed appropriate at first. Big Boy was a pig after all. But I finally decided that the risks were too high.

I settled on disposal in a local river that I'd used once before – a convenient tidal stretch of water that flows into the sea via a beautiful estuary overlooked by a twelfth century Norman castle. I'd got away with it the last time, so why not again? All I had to do was leave the house in the early hours of the morning, drive to a remote spot away from prying eyes, weigh the bags down with suitably sized stones, and drop them into the fast-flowing mix of fresh and saltwater one at a time.

I've decided I'm going to do it tonight. Why delay? I'll be taking another sick day despite my misgivings. Sometimes such things are necessary to serve the bigger picture. I'll let you know how it all goes sometime tomorrow when I'm in the mood to write.

14

Things haven't been easy since writing my previous chapter. My plans, however well intentioned, don't always go as well as I'd hope. And this was one of those times. My endeavours started well enough but it didn't continue that way. My hands are still trembling as I write these words. But I'm determined to continue. My story has to be told.

I preferred driving my own car to Big Boy's vehicle as I headed towards my river of choice. Big Boy had come to me, led to the slaughter, unaware of his impending fate. And now he was butchered and in my car boot, wrapped up in plastic, secured by tape. That had taken some effort on my part. Even after regular weekly exercise, I struggled with the lifting. I was red-faced and panting by the time I finished the process. The packages really were that heavy. There must have been at least fifteen stone of meat, bone and gristle in total. It's not like I can ask anyone for assistance. My poor legs struggled to take the strain.

After a twenty-minute drive deep into the Welsh countryside, I reached the river, a spot where there were no nearby houses to pose any threat. I drove as near the riverbank as possible, manoeuvring carefully through an open farm gate and parking in a snow-covered field behind a high hedge. I realised the task of disposal would be challenging as I looked across the undulating blanket of white. I'd have to climb a second hedge and then trudge another thirty feet or so through several inches of snow to the water.

I took off my hat, scratching my head as I considered the physical effort involved. I tried driving the car on a few yards more. But the wheels span on the frozen ground as I attempted to climb a slight incline, making the task impossible to achieve. The noise of the revving engine worried me greatly, sending my blood pressure soaring to a new and savage high. I feared the sound would carry for miles in the still night air. The last thing I wanted was to draw attention to myself, however remote the area. Being found out was unthinkable. And so I switched off the engine, reluctantly accepting there was no other way but to carry or drag the body parts to the riverbank one heavy parcel at a time. I stifled a scream of frustration, opened the boot, got my head down, and got on with it.

I was glad of my brown leather gloves, another charity shop purchase, and my pair of green wellingtons kept my feet dry. A lesson learnt after my experiences on the beach. The plastic-covered packages slid easily over the frozen ground as I dragged them behind me, except for the head, which I carried in both arms. The shape made the carrying easier, like a ball. And I'd removed the brain, slicing it up for disposal in the sewerage system, which reduced the weight. Something else I'd learnt from experience. I'm becoming more skilled with each killing. I consider that to my credit. Worthy of a symbolic pat on the back.

Things were going reasonably well right up to when I heard a dog bark somewhere in the distance. It set me on edge for some reason I still can't fully quantify. As if it signalled my downfall. As if the animal was prophesying my undoing.

I stood shivering on the bank of the fast-flowing river, the various bloody packages to one side of me and a pile of suitably sized stones to the other. I began placing stones in each parcel one at a time before lowering them into the mire, in turn, watching them slowly sink as they were washed away by the tide. I had two packages left, the head and one leg, when the dog barked again, louder this time, the animal not so far away. I tried to ignore my growing anxiety as I dropped the final leg into the muddy water. But as I turned to pick up the head with shaking hands, a sheepdog suddenly appeared, rushing towards me and snatching Big Boy's plastic-covered head in its jaws. The animal looked at me accusingly as it shook its prize, and then ran off as if to taunt me, the package still clutched in its jaws.

The dog ran along the riverbank with me trying to keep up, running with loping, long bounding steps until I finally fell, grazing a knee and cracking my head against a large, leafless branch of a felled tree. I looked up dazed and tearful as the dog kept running, looking back occasionally because it amused it to do so.

I punched the ground three times before standing, looking for an answer, desperate for revelation, any way of rectifying the situation, but without any hope of success. I spent almost an hour trudging along that riverbank after that, frozen, tearful, increasingly desperate, searching for any sight of the dog or Big Boy's discarded head.

I told myself I'd succeed, that all would come good in the end. But it didn't work out that way. As the sun slowly rose over the distant horizon, I decided the game was up. It was time to go. Time to head home. The risks of being seen were too high and increasing with every minute that passed. But leaving the head was risky too. I could have kept looking. But that's not the decision I made.

I'd never felt more confused or concerned as I drove back

towards my cottage. I'm on the side of the angels. A superhero, the good guy. So why had the universe conspired against me? I couldn't make any sense of it at the time and I still can't now.

I hated that damned dog with a burning intensity that made my head pound. I wanted to kick the animal, to punch it, and drive the life from its body until it returned my property. But that was never going to happen. Not in this world, not in this life; things don't work that way. I had to hope, to rely on random fate.

Say a prayer for me if you feel so inclined. It's something I find difficult to do myself. I need all the help I can get.

15

I don't often watch the Welsh evening news. It doesn't usually interest me. The politics, the Welsh sports reports, and stories of local interest. It's just not my thing. But this evening was different. I was on tenterhooks, agitated, unable to relax even for a moment.

I was desperate for information. Had Big Boy's head been found? And I had other questions too. Questions that dominated my every waking moment. Was my car seen on that cold night as I drove to the river? And were the police on the case? Were they hunting me? Those questions rang in my ears as my father began shouting somewhere behind me. Those same unanswered questions were yelled repeatedly, louder and louder until I feared my head might explode with the force of the sound.

I had to know the reality for good or bad. It was the only way to silence that invasive voice that threatened my sanity.

I switched on the television, turned to the correct channel and waited. I needed to watch. I *had* to watch. If it were bad news, I'd have to deal with it as I had as a child. And as I had since, with one guest after another lured to the slaughter. That's fair, isn't it? I've done well, haven't I? I feel sure you'll support me in that.

My father stopped shouting just as the programme was about to start. He'd timed it to perfection, and I think I know why. I suspect he was hoping I was about to receive bad news. But, of course, I was hoping for no news at all.

I was once told that the anticipation of pain could be worse than the pain itself. The proposition seemed ridiculous to me back then. But I now know it to be true. I tore at my hair as I sat there in front of the television, rocking back and forth in my chair, tapping my foot against the floor. And then there it was on the screen, the lead story, Big Boy's demise was the main headline. *Oh, my God, oh my God! No, no, no!*

I let out an anguished yelp as the pretty, young female journalist continued to present her report. A local farmer had found a man's decapitated head. A head wrapped in black plastic, a head worried by an animal before being discarded close to the river.

I stared at the screen with unblinking eyes, my heart pounding. The presenter didn't mention the missing brain, that didn't feature in the report at all. I still don't know why. But the police were investigating. *Oh my God, they were investigating!* They were attempting to establish the deceased's identity and cause of death. And then the worse news in the world, the very thing I feared the most. The reporter looked into the camera with a manufactured frown to tell all who watched that the case was being treated as a murder.

Shit, shit, shit! My greatest fears were a new reality right there on the screen for all to see. Although, I guess such things were inevitable. If the head was found it would be seen as homicide. How else could he possibly have died?

I felt as if the room was closing in on me. As if the walls were about to fall, crushing me at any moment. The murder investigation would be a high priority case, with no expense spared. I knew that only too well from my work in the probation department. The police would be searching for the killer, snooping, sticking their piggy noses in, looking for *me*. How ridiculous is that given the identity of the victim? And that's if you can call him a victim at all. I should be given a medal. The Queen should pin it on my chest. But that's not the way our sick society works. The wrong people are protected. And so, I need to be *extra* careful from here on in. No more errors, no mistakes. One was one too many.

I stood, turning in a tight circle, my mind still racing, searching for reassurance. I looked for a positive slant, *any* positive slant that would alleviate my concern even slightly. Maybe I wasn't seen, and my car, maybe that wasn't seen either. I'd hidden it well enough in the dead of night. Behind that hedge, in that field covered in snow. My fingerprints weren't on record even if found. And the dog couldn't describe me. Ha! That was obvious. Things weren't that bad, were they? What do you think? You must have a view on the matter. Maybe I am worrying about nothing at all.

I opened a whisky bottle as I paced the room, first one way and then another, pouring the strong liquid down my throat one generous gulp after another. I stopped at the window, tilted my head back and took another swig before staring into the darkness looking for answers. I hoped the alcohol would take the edge off, calm me down a bit, silence that voice in my head. But it didn't really help however much I drank. The strong spirit just clouded my thinking and burnt my throat. So I hurled the three-quarter full bottle at the screen – no more television for me. No more news was good news, wasn't it? I'd lie low for as long as it took to feel safe. That was the sensible thing to do.

If the police turn up snooping, I'll deny everything. It's not so much what I did. It's all about reasonable doubt. Unless they dig up my garden. If they do that I'm screwed. If they prove my *crimes*, I'll have to face whatever punishment the authorities deem appropriate. And if not, I'll continue targeting predators. I could face prison if I have to. I have that inner strength. I've no doubt on that score. It isn't the possibility of incarceration that worries me so very much, not in itself. But there's more offenders out there, some on my shortlist and many not. Men like Big Boy, and some even worse. If I'm not going to stop them, who's going to do it? Can anyone answer that for me? No one, that's the answer, no one, in case you were wondering. I hate that thought. It eats away at me, beats me down.

I fetched the bottle of sleeping draught from a bathroom cupboard. I made my way back downstairs, entered my slaughterhouse for much-needed solace, and curled up on the wooden floor, now free of plastic sheeting for the first time in days. Three gulps of the sweet, green liquid and I was soon drowsy. Only minutes later, I was lost to my chemically induced slumber. I dreamt of mass execution, all my targets there in one room, waiting to die together. Children were safer in one bold move. As if such things were possible; if only they were.

And then I woke up this morning, cold and aching, my back in spasm. My entire body was shaking as I opened my eyes, recalling the events of the evening before. The television report, the whisky, my racing thoughts, my father's voice in my ear.

But there hadn't been a knock on the door. There'd been no sirens disturbing my rest. I reminded myself of those facts as I stretched and stood. It's important to hold on to hope in this world of ours, to focus on the positives whenever you can. I'm still free, not in handcuffs, and that's a triumph in itself. Yes, I have hope, which is more than many can claim.

Maybe I can continue to protect the vulnerable as I have until now. And I will, I definitely will if given the chance. As long as there are predators to hunt. As long as there's breath in my body. As long as I'm not locked up in a cell. Eradicating the dangerous is my reason for living. I'll keep planning. I'll keep searching. And I'll strike again when the time's precisely right. If the police come calling, then so be it, there's little I can do about that. And if not, I'll continue my quest.

16

Over a week has now passed since that evening watching the Welsh evening news, and I'm back at work. Back in an administrative role, but now assisting a senior probation officer, recently promoted, and relatively new in her supervisory role. She rates me, apparently. It's a temporary post while the usual secretary is on maternity leave. She asked me personally. So, how could I say no?

I returned to work in an attempt to seem ordinary. There's been no knock on the door, no police interview, and no arrest. So work seemed like a sensible move to continue my subterfuge. It's a mask of sorts, like that worn by my father. I still jump at every turn of a doorknob, and every passing car, but I think I'm hiding it well. Although, Mrs Breen, that's her name, Maisie Breen, did ask if I were okay at one point this morning. She looked across her small, cluttered office with a quizzical expression and said those exact words.

That concerned me greatly at first. But I resisted my impulse to panic. I explained that the news of the murder had upset me. It was so brutal, so local, so close to home. I said I lived alone, that I didn't feel safe in my own bed – quick thinking on my part, something else to be proud of.

Maisie Breen told me that she understood completely and then opened up over a morning coffee. The sharing of personal information can do that sometimes. It conveys liking. It encourages communication. I've used that to my advantage more than once. She told me she's married to a detective; a man called Rob, one of those on the case. The victim had already been identified utilising his dental records and DNA. No surprises there. He was a sex offender in life, one of the department's many clients.

I feigned surprise, shaking my head slowly when she said that, focusing on the grey carpet at my feet. 'Really? One of ours? How awful!'

'Oh, yes, he was a local paedophile all right. And there's another one missing. The police thought he'd done a runner to avoid supervision. But now they're wondering if he's been murdered too. There may be a vigilante on the loose.'

The second man she talked of is buried in my garden at the back of the cottage along with others. Under a rose bed, manure, food for the worms. I like to think of it as a memorial garden dedicated to their many victims' lost childhoods. I picture those children sometimes when the flowers are in bloom. Happy, laughing children, playing childhood games without a care in the world. As if they'd never encountered a monster. It's all about them. The monsters are rotting in the ground.

'Are you all right, Alice? The colour's drained from your face. I'm sorry if I've said too much. I didn't mean to upset you.'

I refocused on our conversation, pushing my reminiscences from my mind. 'It's just so awful. A murder in a quiet area like ours. Do the police have any idea who the killer is? Will they be arresting someone anytime soon?'

She shook her head forlornly, her voice unchanging in pitch

or tone. 'Not as yet, it's early days; they haven't got a clue. There's going to be a press conference; hopefully, that'll change things.'

I felt my entire body stiffen as I weighed up the possible significance of her statement. 'What's the point of a conference? I don't get it. What are the police trying to achieve?'

Maisie glanced around her before refocusing on me. As if she was revealing the world's greatest secret. 'I probably shouldn't be telling you this, and please keep it to yourself for now. But I guess it will soon be public knowledge anyway. So what possible harm could it do? The head was found on a riverbank, far from any residential dwellings. It had to get there somehow. The police plan to ask the public for help. Someone may have seen something, a person, or a car maybe. They've got nothing else to go on. The press conference is a fishing exercise more than anything else. It's a tactic the police use sometimes, one of many. You never know, they may get lucky.'

I swallowed hard, slowing my breathing as damp patches formed under both my arms. I wanted to stamp and shout and holler. But I stayed in my seat, calming my mood, sipping my hot coffee before speaking again. I'd been surprised by her candour. I'd heard rumours she was a gossip. I'd discounted them at the time. But now I knew it to be true. The woman liked to be liked. Being a new boss didn't suit her at all. I plan to take full advantage of those facts. She gives me a direct link to the investigative team. It seems the universe is on my side after all.

'I really appreciate you sharing, Maisie. Is there anything else you can tell me? It would make me feel so much better if I thought the police are close to catching the killer. Maybe then I could sleep nights.'

She lowered her voice almost to a whisper. 'They found the victim's car on a beach. It was half-submerged in the sea. They've got no idea who drove it there. They'll be appealing for information about that too.'

'Strange!' That's all I could think to say, one single word, how pathetic is that. But it was enough to trigger her continued sharing. I've realised it doesn't take much to get her talking.

'The police are hoping someone saw the car being driven to where it was left. They think it may have something to do with the murder. Rob says it's a hunch more than anything else. A Detective Inspector Kesey is heading up the case, Laura Kesey, she's originally from Birmingham. She's a competent officer. If anyone can catch the killer, she can. She's investigated several previous murders. She's well respected in the force.'

I manufactured an unlikely smile. 'Would you like a biscuit, Maisie? There's some chocolate digestives in the kitchen if you fancy one. I bought them this morning on my way in.'

She checked her office clock, brushing non-existent fluff from her navy skirt as she rose to her feet. 'No, not for me, thanks, I've got a meeting to get to. It's at the police station, as it happens, the Area Child Protection Committee. It's my first one.'

'Best of luck with it.'

She shrugged. 'Oh, I'll be fine. If I hear anything significant, I'll let you know. I like to keep my staff fully informed. We girls have got to stick together.'

I really couldn't believe my luck. I'd hit the information jackpot. Her mouth runs away with her, how fortunate is that! 'Quite right too. Do you happen to know when the press conference is happening? I'd really like to watch it if I can.'

She picked up a black leather briefcase, preparing to leave. 'It's tomorrow afternoon. They'll be talking about it on the Welsh evening news, BBC Wales Today. I think it starts at half past six.'

I nodded once. 'Thanks, Maisie, I'll have to check it out.'

She looked back on approaching the exit. 'I'll see you in the morning. I won't be back today. There are things I need to do. You've got my mobile number if there's anything urgent.'

I waved with feigned enthusiasm as my new boss placed her hand on the door handle. A black cloud had descended. It suddenly felt as if events were spiralling out of my control as I sat there alone in that room. I heard my father's mocking voice as clear as day. As if he was there with me.

Did you hear that, Alice? Did you hear what your new friend said? There's going to be a press conference. Oh, dear, how very unfortunate! What if someone saw you? What if that someone rings the police? Your world would come crashing down. One stupid mistake and it could all be over. That's all down to you, my girl. Consider your failings and weep.

I covered my ears as a world of pain exploded in my head. 'Shut up, you vile creature. Shut the fuck up!'

But he didn't go away. *You won't silence me, however hard you try. I'll haunt you forever.*

I closed my eyes tight shut and started humming. 'You're dead; you can't hurt me anymore.'

You're such a mess, Alice, such a screw-up. Do you really think you can escape me?

'Get out of my life! I don't care what you say. All I can do is wait. Maybe it's over, and maybe it's not. That's not for you to decide.'

17

I replaced my television set at a reasonable cost after taking the old one to the local tip for recycling. I'm trying to stay busy. It helps stop me overthinking. And looking after the ecology of the planet should be a priority. The more flowers I'm able to plant, the better for everyone. And so my rose garden serves two useful purposes, it's a win-win. Once again I'm trying to stay positive as I make my contributions to humanity.

The Welsh news report was now only half an hour away. I could ignore it. I could trust in random fate. But I've always been at the centre of events. That's what I told myself. I'm an activist, not a follower, pulling strings as I did on that clifftop, sending the monster man crashing to the rocks in the cold sea below. If I'm going to go down, I'll go down fighting. I'll watch that report, and I'll assess the likely consequences. I'll do everything I can to alleviate any risks I face to the very best of my ability. Not for my sake, but for the sake of the children; if my vocational activities come crashing down as my father so vehemently predicted, it won't be for the lack of trying on my part. A quick drink and I'll be ready for the watching, seated and waiting, staring at the screen with the volume turned up. I've decided there's no room for denial. I'll deal with whatever comes full on, no hiding behind the sofa or covering my eyes. I'll take whatever comes and prepare for the fight.

Big Boy's story formed the majority of the programme. That didn't surprise me at all. It's not every day a monster's head is discovered in the Welsh countryside. It was always going to get some attention once it was found. And that's down to me. If I'd done my job right, it wouldn't have been found at all. It's not all about the killing. Disposal is almost as important. I got careless, lazy. I won't make that mistake again if given a chance.

The conference started with DI Laura Kesey seated facing a room full of journalists, some with notepads and others with cameras. She was wearing a smart charcoal-grey trouser suit with a crisp white blouse that complemented it perfectly. An outfit that I strongly suspect was intended to convey both authority and efficiency. Her dyed black hair was short and neat, not unlike mine, although, of course, mine is a rather nice shade of brown. She wasn't wearing much make-up, just the basics. I don't think she's vain by nature. She looked slightly on edge as if the prospect of addressing the public caused her some anxiety. I liked that about her. It was something I could relate to. She's a woman like me – a female in a male-dominated world. And we're both on the side of the innocent. It seems we're not so very different after all.

Kesey introduced a Detective Sergeant Raymond Lewis who was seated next to her. He's an older, heavier individual, a little out of shape with a salt and pepper beard that's much in need of trimming. He looked world-worn but relaxed, a follower, not a leader, a career sergeant comfortable in his own skin. There was a large force logo on the white painted wall behind the two officers. I won't name the force for obvious reasons. Some things are best kept secret in the interests of my freedom.

Kesey talked of Big Boy's car first, saying where it was found and when, and then moving on to ask for the public's help. You know the sort of thing. If anyone saw the car at the relevant time or had any other information pertinent to the case, they should contact the police, who'd be ready and waiting. Those weren't her exact words, but they're pretty damned close.

DS Lewis flicked a switch, presenting a large colour photo of the car in question on the white painted wall to the right side of the logo. I took a deep breath, sucking in the fetid air, fearing my father may make an unwelcome appearance at any second with one negative comment or another. But for once the bastard didn't materialise either inside or outside my head. Please don't ask me why. I have no way of knowing. Sometimes he does, and other times he doesn't. It's another of life's mysteries.

DI Kesey moved to the front of a table topped with a white cloth, walking towards the TV camera and looking directly into the lens. Now it was time to talk of murder, as her sergeant flicked that same switch for a second time. The wall now displayed a large mugshot of Big Boy taken when in the land of the living. The very sight of the monster man made me want to puke up my dinner. He was evil personified, the devil up there on the police headquarters wall. And yet there was no talk of his crimes, just the fact of his marriage and fatherhood.

That angered me to the point of exasperation. And why call it murder? Execution would have been a far more suitable term. I rose to my feet and battered the wall with the sides of both fists until I reached exhaustion. Is it only me that cares about children? *Ahhh!* What the fuck is wrong with humanity? It was as if Big Boy's many victims didn't matter at all.

Another appeal for information followed as I sunk to the floor like a punch-drunk fighter hitting the canvas. I lay there clutching my vodka bottle for another half hour or so, intermittently gulping the contents until the bottle was empty. I slept in my slaughterhouse again that night for the consolation it offered in a time of distress – this time in a sleeping bag to keep out the cold.

As I drove to work the next morning, my head was thumping, as much from the fear of potential discovery as from alcoholic excess. If the police have a witness, I'll soon know about it. And if not, I've been lucky. I've no way of knowing which direction my life will now take. I have no option but to wait to find out if it's freedom or prison that awaits me. I can only recount something I once said to my father. Only time will tell.

18

I think they call it introspection, the examination and observation of one's life. I've been pondering my actions, assessing my behaviour while I have the time to think. Recent months have been taken up with planning and targeting; with the destruction and disposal of vermin. Activities I've had to put on reluctant hold until the sudden interest in my deeds abates.

And so I've looked back on each of my executions. I won't call them murders, because each killing was justified. Each man was a predator, an abuser of children. Someone had to stop them, and that someone was me. I take pride in that achievement and feel no regret or guilt. Some suffered horribly, and others died quickly. I still don't think that's unreasonable given the facts of each case. Every punishment was proportionate and done for good reason. No more or less than each criminal deserved.

I don't think of myself as a psychopath, or in any way, evil. I want to make that crystal clear and I hope you agree. I feel empathy for others, just not for the world's predators. It's not my needs that matter but those of the children. And so, in conclusion, I'm committed to continuing my clandestine activities. I'll just put off the next execution until the time feels right. In the meantime, it's all about retaining my freedom. I'll duck, and I'll dive and see where I get to. And with that said I'll get on with my tale.

Today was Maisie's birthday, her thirty-fifth, a cause for celebration. I think she looks a little older, but I won't burst her bubble. There's nothing to be gained by a lack of sensitivity. If I can't say something nice, I'll say nothing at all.

I called at a petrol station on my way into work this morning, dodging the raindrops as I ran from the car. I bought the birthday girl a card and a small box of milk chocolates. A worthwhile investment intended to solidify our friendship. She'll have more to tell me as a result of her pillow talk. Information I can use. Given my circumstances, I need all the help I can get.

I parked my car at the probation office and entered the building as the rain got heavier, large droplets of water bouncing off the ground around my feet. I took my wet coat off before entering the kitchen, where I made Maisie a coffee, adding powdered milk to her taste. For some reason, she likes it that way, and it suits me to please her. I'll repeat the process willingly and often if it helps me to win.

I knocked on Maisie's office door with her favourite blue mug in one hand and her gifts in the other, pushing the door open with the point of my shoe. She smiled warmly as soon as she saw me, putting down her office phone, ending her call. I placed each item on her teak-veneered desk and said happy birthday. She smiled again without parting her lips this time, waved a hand in a welcoming gesture, and said to pull up a chair.

Maisie opened her card, sipped her hot drink after blowing it, and then offered me a chocolate, which I politely declined due to a lactose intolerance. Milk and anything containing it, even in the smallest of quantities, causes havoc with my digestive system and is best avoided. Something else I shared with her to encourage her to talk.

After about five minutes of pointless chit-chat, she asked the question I was waiting for. Waiting in trepidation as we continued to talk.

'Did you see the highlights of the press conference?'

I nodded, asking myself which direction the conversation was about to take. Would it be good or bad news or no news at all? Whichever it was, I knew I had to hear the truth. 'Yeah, I did, I watched all of it. You were right; I thought DI Kesey was *really* impressive. I didn't think that much of her sergeant though. Now, there's a man who needs a good makeover. Did the police gain any relevant information as a result of the appeal?'

I could see from her face that she couldn't wait to tell me the answer. But she delayed her response, upping my anticipation. Like on one of those ridiculous talent shows I choose not to watch. You know the ones I'm talking about.

'Yes, they did, as it happens. A witness phoned in shortly after the programme ended. A man in his early eighties who claimed to have seen the dead man's car being driven close to the beach where it was found at the relevant time. My Rob interviewed him and took a statement late last night. The witness described a *woman* driving the car, a woman wearing a hat and glasses. He wasn't sure of her age. Can you believe that? Everyone was expecting it to be a man.'

My eyes bounced from one part of the room to another. I could feel the sweat forming on my brow. I could sense my face reddening as my temperature rose. *A witness, a fucking witness!*

'Are you okay, Alice? You don't look very well all of a sudden. Can I get you a glass of water?'

What to say? What the hell to say? I felt as if I was caught in a waking nightmare. A whirlpool of despair threatened to drag me down. I sat there as if under a spotlight, all the attention on me. Perhaps driving the car to the sea had been stupid. Maybe I'd blown it. I resisted the temptation to bolt for the door. I had to say something. Sitting there in silence wasn't an option at all. 'This, um, this is probably going to sound ridiculous. But I couldn't sleep that night. I was worried about my sister. She, er, she hasn't been well. I went out for a long drive ending up at the coast. I'm *certain* I saw that car too, the one featured in the press conference, but driven by a man, *definitely* not a woman.'

Maisie pulled her head back, eyes wide, the whites flashing. 'Are you sure?'

I nodded frantically, moving to the very edge of my chair with my hands resting on my knees for effect. 'Yes, I'm absolutely certain of it, I've never been more certain of anything in my life.'

'Have you contacted the police?'

How could I answer that? 'No, I wanted to talk to you first.'

That was the best I could offer. I know it didn't make a great deal of sense, but for some reason she failed to challenge me. I was pleased with my quick thinking. Maybe Maisie took my explanation as a compliment, her ego boosted. I think that was probably it. I've come to learn that it doesn't take much to flatter her. She is so in need of validation. She laps it up every chance she gets.

'Right, I'll tell you what I'm going to do. I'm going to telephone my Rob, and I'm going to tell him exactly what you've told me. It's crucial information. The police need to know.'

'Okay, if you think that's for the best.'

She looked back at me a little sheepishly, peeping over the top of her reading glasses. 'I do, Alice, I do. But please don't share how much I've told you. Don't mention you know of another witness. I probably shouldn't have said anything. Keep that to yourself.'

I smiled warmly as she began dialling. 'I won't say a thing; mum's the word.'

I listened intently as Maisie spoke to her partner. I only heard one side of the conversation, but I was still able to make sense of most of it. She looked across at me on putting the phone down, her tone was urgent, her body tense.

'Rob's going to speak to Laura Kesey straight away. You can expect a phone call sometime this morning. You'll need to make a written statement. It really is important. This isn't a time for delay.'

I rose to my feet, pleased with developments. I had the opportunity to misdirect the police investigation. I saw that as a major positive. I'd have to hold my nerve, of course, and stick as close to the truth as possible. And I'd have to tell the police what I needed them to hear, just as I did as a child. If I could do it then, I could again. It was a case of repeating the past.

'Thank you, Maisie, you've been brilliant. I don't know what I'd do without you. You're the best boss a girl could have.'

19

I only had to sit and wait, twiddling my thumbs, playing with my cuff, for about ten minutes before my office phone rang out, making me jump. I fingered my bead necklace with one hand as I held the phone to my face, confirming my identity following DI Kesey's introduction. She quickly confirmed what Maisie had told Rob and then asked me to come to the police station where she would interview me personally.

I asked, 'When?'

And the DI replied, 'Now.'

Just that one word and I was on my way. Within a few minutes, I was driving out of the probation office car park, onto the main road, and turning left towards the police station on the other side of town. It had all happened so very quickly in the end, and my initial confidence was starting to wane ever so slightly. It was so very different to when I'd been a teenager. It felt as if there was much more at stake now. Maybe a bit of me was enjoying the killings. That thought troubled me as I drove on. Such things are so confusing. Perhaps it was the stress that was getting to me. It was so very hard to get my thoughts straight in my head.

My chest tightened as the traffic slowed in front of my car. My meeting with Kesey was going to be pivotal. I had to be convincing. My evidence had to be compelling. I had to contradict their elderly witness and do it well. Nothing less was acceptable. There was far too much to lose.

Kesey was waiting to greet me in reception when I entered the modernist building. She reached out, shaking my hand warmly with a surprisingly firm grip. She spoke in that same Midlands tone I'd heard on the television. 'Thank you for coming so quickly, Alice, your co-operation is appreciated.'

I smiled, keen to appear friendly and relaxed. I did not want to seem in any way ill at ease. Nothing to suggest I was anything other than a reliable witness. 'It was the least I could do in the circumstances. I'm delighted to help if I can. It's a horrible case.'

The detective was quick to respond as she took a backward step, looking me in the eye. 'So, why not contact us sooner? Why the delay?'

That unnerved me. Was she suspicious or merely inquisitive? I still don't know the answer to that one. I should have anticipated the question. I had to think fast. 'A migraine came on as I was watching the news report. It's a regular affliction. I took some strong painkillers prescribed by my doctor. They made me feel drowsy. It's an unfortunate side effect. I went for a lie-down and didn't wake up again until morning.'

The detective tilted her head at a slight angle, studying me, her expression suddenly softening as if she'd accepted my explanation as reasonable. Or, at least, that's how I read it at the time. 'All the interview rooms are in use. You're here as a witness. There's no need for formality; if you follow me, we can talk in my office.'

I talked as I walked, following her towards the lift. 'Are you any nearer to catching the killer?'

She chose to ignore my enquiry, which didn't surprise me in the slightest. It's a tactic the police sometimes use. It gives them power. I saw it in a true-crime documentary some months back.

'How long have you worked for the probation service?'

That was one I could answer without any difficulty. 'I've been there since completing my degree course a couple of years ago.'

Kesey led the way into her second-floor office, holding the door open for me to enter first. It was a small, brightly lit room, with a single window overlooking the car park: nothing remarkable, just a workplace like any other. 'Take a seat, Alice, and we'll make a start.'

I noted a silver-framed photo of a woman and a young boy on her desk as I pulled up a chair. The child looked about five or six years of age. It was a happy photo. I pointed at it with a smile. 'Family?'

She nodded, her head moving only slightly. 'Right, let's make a start. I need you to tell me everything you saw, and I do mean *everything*. This is a murder investigation. The detail matters.'

My seat was padded with a suitably shaped backrest, but I couldn't get comfortable. 'I don't know where to start.'

'How about at the beginning? I usually find that's best.' She appeared to be losing patience. I needed to up my game.

'Well, it's exactly as I told Maisie. I went to bed early that night, but I couldn't sleep. My little sister has been unwell. It was playing on my mind. I hate to think of her suffering.'

Kesey picked up a pen. 'Okay, so you got up, what happened next?'

'I made myself some herbal tea, camomile with a little honey to help me unwind, and then I went out for a drive. I do sometimes when I'm stressed. It helps me to relax.'

'Where did you drive to?'

This was it. This bit mattered. We were getting to the crux of my story. 'I ended up at the coast, at the beach resort where the dead man's car was found.'

'And you claim you saw it?'

I replied immediately. 'Oh, yes, I did. There's no doubt in my mind.'

'What's your eyesight like after dark?'

'It's excellent, it always has been.'

'Were you wearing glasses?'

I pressed my knees together to stop myself shaking. 'I wear contact lenses, never glasses, I don't find them comfortable.'

She appeared to be studying the bridge of my nose. 'Okay, I want you to think *very* carefully. Are you *certain* it was the car we're interested in? Couldn't it have been a similar one? It's a common model.'

Two questions in one. Both of which were hard to answer with conviction. 'I parked immediately in front of it, near to the ramp that goes down onto the sand. I know what I saw.'

'That doesn't explain why you're so sure.'

'It was the number plate, the fifty-two, that's my lucky number. I took it as a good omen. You know, as if God was sending me a sign that my sister's going to be okay. I know that probably sounds ridiculous to you. But it's how it was.'

The detective looked less than convinced. 'Did you see the driver?'

My left eye began to twitch. I reached up, touching my face to stop it. Kesey was asking questions she already knew the answer to. But why? Was she trying to catch me out? What the hell? Maybe, it was a definite possibility. This interview wasn't nearly as easy as that with the nice officer following my father's death. 'Oh, yes, I had a *very* clear view of him. I was no more than twenty feet away. And he'd stopped the car under a street lamp.'

Kesey cleared her throat. 'Okay, now this *really* matters. You said *him*, not her, *him*. Are you certain the person you saw driving that car was a man?'

As soon as she asked that question, I knew I was winning. 'One hundred per cent, I couldn't be more sure, I've got no doubt in my mind. There was a man in the driver's seat. There is no way it was a woman.'

I could tell it wasn't the answer she was hoping for. The police hate inconsistencies. It was written all over her face. But she had to accept my verbal statement if I drove it home. I was credible; I'm sure of that. I didn't have a police record, not even a parking ticket. And I was a graduate who worked for the probation service.

'Was there anyone else in the car?'

'No, just the one man, the one behind the wheel.'

She raised her eyes to the ceiling. 'Can you describe him for me?'

Oh, yes! Things were going my way. I described my father. I could picture him clearly. The second useful thing he'd done in his life.

The detective inspector made some notes. 'Is there anything else you can tell me about the driver before we move on?'

'No, I've got nothing to add.'

Next Kesey clarified the times. She asked me what time I'd left my cottage that night, what time I'd arrived at the beach, what time I'd seen the car, and what time I left to drive home.

I told her what I needed her to hear.

'And you're *sure* it was that night? Could it have been another date? If you've got any doubts, any doubts at all, now's the time to tell me. No one's going to hold it against you.'

I met the officer's gaze and shook my head. 'I've told you what happened. And I truly hope it's helpful. The thought of a deranged killer roaming the Welsh countryside is truly terrifying. The quicker you catch the madman, the happier I'll be.'

Kesey sighed as she took a statement form from a desk drawer. 'Okay, I think that's it for now. Let's get a statement down on paper.'

20

I arranged a girls' night out with Maisie the following Friday. I would like to have met with her sooner, but she said she only socialised at weekends because of work.

We met at an atmospheric Indian restaurant that's popular with locals. You know the sort of place I'm talking about: warm, vibrant colours and layers of texture, beckoning visitors to come in and get comfortable. It's called the Taj Mahal which seems to suit it perfectly. There are large, brightly coloured paintings of the iconic monument on two of the four walls. The restaurant has won an award for the quality of its food. Or, at least, that's what the certificate says in the front window. It's a bit faded now that I think about it. So it could say just about anything at all. Not that it matters. I was there to solicit information, not to enjoy a convivial meal.

Maisie was already seated at a table for two when I entered the restaurant a little after seven that evening. She looked so very different from when we're in work, less formal with more make-up, long lashes, dark mascara making her eyes pop, and bright scarlet lipstick highlighting her mouth.

I, in contrast, hadn't made much of an effort at all. I felt dowdy by comparison as I waved to greet her. But it hardly mattered. I have no interest in the males of our species, not in a sexual way. My new boss is very different, and I'm grateful for that. No Rob would mean no information. Without him, I wouldn't have been in the restaurant at all. I sat down opposite her, the first to talk. I wanted to run the show. 'You're looking nice tonight, very glamorous. What a lovely dress!'

Maisie sipped her wine, a house white. 'What, this old thing? I've had it for ages.'

'Well, you look wonderful.' I was wearing a pair of old white trainers, blue jeans and a charity shop jumper. What could she possibly say in return?

'It's nice to see you away from the office.'

Ah, so she had some tact. I nodded enthusiastically. 'Yes, sometimes you just click with someone. It's been good to get to know you better. You've become a friend as well as my manager. I'm sure we're going to have a lovely evening.'

Maisie smiled warmly, revealing cosmetically enhanced teeth which looked excessively white even in the dim lighting. I couldn't understand how I hadn't noticed them before. Maybe it was the scarlet lipstick – that dramatic contrast. The colour reminded me of blood.

She picked up her glass. 'Are you going to join me?'

I wanted her drunk and me sober – anything to loosen her tongue. 'Maybe just the one, I'll be driving home.'

'Rob dropped me off. He's good like that. He calls himself my taxi service.'

I forced a laugh that sounded strange even to me. 'Lucky you; make the most of it. You deserve it.'

She handed me a menu, pushing it across the table before picking another up herself – a couple of minutes passed with us both perusing the many meals on offer. There were so many options, but I knew exactly what I wanted. Maisie was the first to lay her menu back on the table. I was keen to give her the illusion of control.

She said she would have the lamb pasanda with pilau rice and onion bhajis. And then she asked if I was ready to order.

I replied in the affirmative. I always have the same thing, a mild vegetable curry with plain, boiled rice. I'm not a meat-eater. Does that surprise you? Some may see it as a contradiction. But I don't see it that way. I'm a lover of animals. I didn't need to look at the menu at all.

We engaged in worthless gossip until our food finally arrived about twenty minutes later. Maisie had drunk three glasses of wine by that time, with my encouragement to consume more. I poured my wine back into the half-empty carafe when she made a brief toilet visit. She didn't register it at all.

Maisie ordered a lager when she returned to our table, claiming it better suited her spicy fare. She was probably right, and I may have joined her in different circumstances. But I ordered water and stuck to that. With each drink, she became louder and less discreet. When she began talking of her sex life, I knew the time was right to redirect the conversation to my advantage. I lowered my head, took a paper tissue from a trouser pocket, and began dabbing at each of my eyes in turn.

'What's wrong, Alice? I hope I haven't said something to upset you.'

I screwed up my face. 'No, it's just the murder case. It's so awful. I can't stop thinking about it. I've got a horrible feeling I didn't help the police at all.'

'What on earth has given you that idea? Rob says DI Kesey's relieved you spoke to her when you did. The old guy he interviewed sent the investigation in *completely* the wrong direction. Rob compared it to the Yorkshire Ripper case. You know, when that idiot man sent a tape in claiming to be the killer. Rob doesn't think the old guy lied. But it would have had much the same negative effect on the investigation if it wasn't for your evidence. You really did save the day.'

I returned the tissue to my pocket with a thin smile. 'Really?'

'Oh, yes, absolutely, you may well have described the killer.'

And then I said something foolish. I revealed my true feelings like never before. How very stupid was that? Right there in that restaurant. I'm sure my absent father would have loved it. Was he there in the room, watching his idiot daughter dig a deep hole for herself before jumping right in? I see things in black and white, simple, uncomplicated, with no shades of grey. I sometimes forget that not everyone does.

'At least our killer only murders nonces. Would it *really* matter if he killed a few more?'

Maisie pulled her head back, spilling the little that was left of her drink onto the tablecloth. '*Alice!* I can't believe you said that.'

I should have shut my ridiculous mouth right there and then without saying another word. But for some reason, I didn't. What a stupid girl! Maybe my father was correct all along.

'At least it would save us the hassle of supervising the perverts.'

Maisie sat back in her chair, folding her arms across her chest. She had a sour expression on her face for the first time that evening. You could have cut the atmosphere with a knife. 'I'm going to pretend that you didn't say that. We're not in work, so I'm going to ignore it. But I don't *ever* want to hear you say something like that again.'

I bit my tongue hard. It was the only way I could silence myself. I tried to laugh. But I couldn't force the sound from my mouth. 'I'm so very sorry, Maisie, I was playing devil's advocate. What I said didn't reflect my true feelings, not in the slightest. Honestly, it didn't, I was being provocative, that's all. I just wanted to know what *you* thought. Your opinion really matters to me.'

She relaxed slightly but only slightly. 'Are you sure that's true?'

I held my hands out wide, my fingers spread. 'We're friends; I wouldn't say it if it weren't. Our relationship means far too much to me to damage it with lies. The truth is, I'd like to do *more* work with sex offenders. I want to contribute to changing their behaviour as you do. You're my heroine, and I want to be like you. I may even study for my probation practice diploma. I think I could do it with your help.'

She burped at full volume and grinned. The alcohol was working its magic. 'Wow, I've never been an inspiration before. And as for becoming a probation officer. You're *more* than capable. And I'd support you every step of the way. It sounds like a marvellous idea.'

'I'd love you to be my mentor. Will you help me learn?'

She gestured to a waiter, ordering more alcohol before formulating her reply. 'How about we start as we mean to go on? How would you feel about sitting in on a multi-agency risk assessment meeting next week?'

'Oh, yes, please, that sounds fascinating.'

'A high-risk offender named Arthur Simpson is being released on licence on the third of next month. He's served half of a sixteen-year sentence for child rape. He's completed the sex offender programme. He's fully co-operated, accepted responsibility for his past crimes, and is being released early for good behaviour. The parole board made the decision. They believe he's a changed man.'

Like fuck he is! I thought, but kept my mouth shut. It seemed wise.

Maisie stalled, raised her glass to her mouth, drank, and smiled again before continuing. 'Am I coming on a bit strong?

What with all this work talk. It's Friday night. We're supposed to be enjoying ourselves.'

'No, no, not at all, I'm finding everything you're saying incredibly interesting. Please tell me more.'

'Okay, if you're sure?'

'I'm fascinated by this stuff, the complexities of offending behaviour. People's capacity to change. And you're the expert.'

She beamed. 'There's a meeting at the local social services office at eleven o'clock on Wednesday morning to discuss Simpson's supervision. I can ask the chairperson if you can observe if you'd like me to. You wouldn't actually be taking part in the meeting. You'd be there to watch and listen. But it may give you a better idea if the work is for you.'

'Oh, thanks so very much, Maisie. I'd love that. You're an absolute star.'

Maisie grinned. 'Glad to be of service.'

'Do you really think the chair will agree to me being there?'

She winked, can you believe that? The silly cow actually winked at me, right there across the table. What a ridiculous woman, so full of herself, so pumped up with her importance.

'Yes, it won't be a problem. I've known him for ages. I think he fancies me.'

I reached across the table to squeeze her perfectly manicured hand, holding it gently for a second or two before withdrawing my arm. 'I am *so* fortunate to have a boss like you.'

Maisie's resulting smile lit up her face. It was that easy. She was putty in my hands. And I a puppeteer pulling her strings. But then she surprised even me. 'Why don't you sleep at my place tonight? We could have a *proper* drink together. Maybe even go to a club. There's a good one in the high street I used to go to as a teenager. I do love a boogie.'

The very idea of a busy club filled me with dread. Not so much the dancing, but all those sweaty people in one dark room. There could be anyone in there – any number of dangers. But, of course, I was never going to tell Maisie that, not then, not ever. I poured myself a glass of wine and drained it before pouring another. My aims for the evening were already achieved. Why not numb my troubled mind for a time? I'd been drinking more alcohol in recent weeks, as I did in my college days. It still didn't seem to help a great deal, as it hadn't then. But maybe now it would take the edge off if I drank enough. If I poured sufficient quantities down my eager throat. I decided it had to be worth a try as I heard my father's voice chattering in my ear for the first time that evening.

'Oh, what the hell, go on then, as long as your Rob's not going to mind me staying. Let's get *seriously* drunk together. We'll have a right laugh. I can collect my car in the morning.'

21

Maisie rushed me into her office when I arrived in work on the Tuesday morning, closing the door with a bang as soon as I sat myself down. I usually make a coffee first thing. It sets me up for the day. But it seemed even that was out of the question. It was as if she'd won the national lottery. I'd never seen the woman so animated, never so full of great enthusiasm and eagerness. She was desperate to share. And it suited me to listen.

'Grab a seat, Alice. You are not going to believe this.'

I craned my neck toward her. I didn't need to feign interest. I really was curious as to what she had to say. 'Okay, I'm all ears.'

'A man's *hand* was found at the local tip on Sunday afternoon.'

Oh, shit! That wasn't good. It wasn't good at all. You're probably going to think I've been careless when I explain what had happened. And I wouldn't blame you if you do. I chose to feign ignorance. It was the best card I had to play. 'Did it belong to the same man as the head?'

She crossed and uncrossed her legs. Not an easy task in her over-tight skirt. 'No, that's what the police thought at first. Rob said Kesey arranged urgent lab tests and fingerprints. It doesn't belong to the same man at all.'

I nodded knowingly. 'Ah, yeah, right, I bet you're going to tell me that the missing paedophile you mentioned has been murdered too, probably by the same killer.'

'Yes, you'd think that, wouldn't you? The police thought it too. But it seems not. It's someone else entirely. They still haven't identified the victim. There's a small tattoo of a red dragon on the hand. I've been trying to think if that describes any of our clients.'

'Surely he'd be on record if he was one of ours, DNA, fingerprints and the like.'

'Yes, yes, of course, he would. I wasn't thinking. It's been a long night. Rob's phone kept ringing. I didn't get much sleep.'

I knew exactly who the hand belonged to – one of my previous guests who'd arrived at the cottage in the summer. The artwork had interested me. There was something about it that I'd liked. I'd finally thrown the hand out after some time in my freezer. I don't know why. Maybe it was the alcohol. What the hell was I thinking? I've rarely disposed of body parts in that way before. And now I'd done it again at the worst possible time.

'Does that mean there may be three dead men?'

Maisie nodded her agreement.

'That is *exactly* what it means. The police suspect they're dealing with a serial killer, here, on our patch. Rob says it's a man who hates sex offenders. Someone who's probably from this area and knows it well. The police call it the killer's *zone of comfort*. They are even talking about involving a profiler. There's a guy who worked for the FBI who Kesey is planning to talk to. Can you believe it? It's the sort of thing you see on the telly.'

'Shall I put the kettle on? I can't stop shaking. I think we need something to prepare for the day.'

Maisie blew the air from her mouth. 'Yes, why not? Make mine a strong one, plenty of coffee.'

'And a biscuit?'

'Yes, what the hell, I could do with a treat. I think I may be in shock after everything that Rob told me. To think we might *know* the killer. Can you imagine? It could be someone we've seen in town, even a neighbour. These people are sometimes the last person you'd suspect.'

'It's a pity they don't come with a warning stamped on their foreheads.'

Maisie grinned but didn't comment as I stood to leave the room. The silly mare really would be in shock if she knew the truth. She was looking for the executioner in all the wrong places. She wouldn't recognise fairness if it jumped up and bit her on her fat arse, sank in its teeth and chewed out a chunk. The thought amused me no end as I stood in the kitchen waiting for the kettle to come to the boil. I wish I could have told her of my secret activities with pride and passion. I wish she were the sort of woman who'd give me the credit I deserve. I'd like to shout it out for all to hear. Why doesn't the world celebrate my contribution? I know I've asked that question before, but I still don't have an answer. If those in power had more sense, I'd be given a thousand plaudits. People would be cheering for me in the streets. But instead, I've got to hide in the shadows. As if there's something intrinsically wrong with what I do. Where's the justice in that?

I returned to Maisie's office a few minutes later with two mugs of hot coffee and a plate of biscuits on an old tin tray. 'There you go, just as you like it.'

She looked up from her paperwork. 'Thanks, Alice, much appreciated as always.'

'Did you have a chance to speak to the guy you mentioned? The one who's chairing the Simpson meeting?'

Maisie dunked a biscuit into her coffee before eating, talking with her mouth full. 'Yes, it's all done. There's not going to be a problem. It took a bit of persuasion, but he agreed in the end.'

'That's brilliant; I had a horrid feeling he was going to say no.'

'Some of the things discussed at the meeting may be a bit difficult for you to hear. But I think you're up to it. You're made of strong stuff.'

I prepared to leave. I didn't think she had anything else useful to say. 'You'll be there if I need you, that's good enough for me.'

Maisie picked up a sheaf of papers and smiled. 'Thanks for the coffee, Alice. I'd better get on.'

So unhelpful, so dismissive, I liked her a little less after that comment. Or was I being unreasonable? I find such things hard to judge sometimes. Not that it matters. She's so easy to please.

I'll tell you how the risk assessment meeting goes after it's happened. The more information I can glean, the better for me. That's how I see it. It seems things may be going my way after all.

22

The day of the risk assessment meeting came, and still no arrest for murder, not of me or anyone else. I was still free, with not even a hint of police attention. There'd been no knock on my door, no interview under caution, not as much as an accusing look. Maybe my self-inflicted downtime wasn't necessary in the first place. Perhaps I'd overreacted to events all along.

In conclusion, I'd already decided that the time was right to target another offender. I could no longer see any reason for delay. I still had my shortlist. I had someone in mind. I'd even considered how best to kill him. I was itching to get my hands on the bastard. But the day of the meeting was a day that would change everything. The information I'd glean would prove pivotal, both for Simpson and for me. That's the way life is sometimes. We're swept along by the tide.

Maisie did the driving as we headed to the meeting. Her car's faster than mine, more comfortable, and no doubt a lot more expensive too. It's a shiny silver German convertible with a folding metal roof, which seems attractive on the face of it. But I soon concluded that it wouldn't suit me at all even if I could afford it. I quite liked the idea of readily available sunshine and fresh air in the warmer summer months. But there's no boot space for a body. And that would be a problem. Such a car just wouldn't be practical. It wouldn't meet my needs at all.

I sat next to Maisie, glad of my seat belt, clutching my seat with both hands as we whizzed through the morning traffic, on the way to the social services office, where the meeting would be held. Maisie seemed oblivious to the dangerous nature of her driving as she explained the relevant procedures in that animated way of hers. She talked and talked, lording over me and playing the expert as if I knew nothing at all. I closed my eyes more than once, fearing a sudden impact as she dodged one vehicle after another. But she appeared strangely relaxed, at times driving with only one hand on the steering wheel, right up to the time we arrived at our destination about ten minutes later. After failing to find a space in the office car park, we left the car in the street and hurried towards the building to escape the winter cold. I felt like dancing as I went. It was partly relief at arriving safely, and partly anticipation that so raised my mood. Being there that day was so much better than sitting in the probation office. I was there as an observer, but it hardly mattered. I would be at the centre of things and saw that as progress. I was excited as to what the day would bring.

Maisie led the way into the large red brick building. I was glad of the relative warmth that met me at the door. As we entered the conference room, several professionals were already seated and waiting, although we were early rather than late. It seemed they were all almost as keen as I was to take part. Either that or they had nothing better to do.

The meeting was chaired by a man named Nicholson. The same one who'd agreed to me being there. He's a social work child protection manager who looks as if he's in his late thirties or early forties. He was quite good looking, with dark brown hair, a short beard, and aviator glasses that are no longer in fashion. Not that his looks interested me a great deal – it's an observation in the interest of detail – although his calm efficiency did. It was apparent to me that all the attending professionals knew one another.

They smiled and talked as we sat in a circle, the room full of chatter until the chairman raised a hand in the air about five minutes later. All were silenced in an instant. It seemed the chairman had a quiet authority they respected. He's a lucky man in that regard; if only it were the same for me.

Nicholson introduced himself; I suspect more for my benefit than anything else. There are good guys out there in this world of ours, and I think he's probably one of them. Not every man is a monster. You've just got to work out which men are which. I may have mentioned that all men should come with either good or bad stamped on their foreheads. The world would be a safer place if they did.

Nicholson asked each of the other attendees to introduce themselves in turn. I was grateful for that. Most were strangers to me if not to each other. Words can be dangerous, but they can also be welcoming. And I felt welcomed as he explained the reason for my attendance. He asked the attendee's agreement, stating it needed to be unanimous, and thankfully no one objected. If they'd known my real purpose, it could have been very different. But my secrets were safe.

I looked at each person in turn, smiled and thanked them for their generosity. My words were genuine. I really was pleased. There was Maisie, of course, that goes without saying, a social worker, a headteacher, a GP, a health visiting manager, a senior prison officer, a uniformed police inspector, a criminal psychologist, and finally a local authority solicitor, and little old me.

It seemed the minute-taker hadn't turned up due to a last-minute family crisis. Maisie, who was seated immediately next to me, offered my services. She didn't ask me, she just blurted it out, as if my opinion didn't matter at all. As if I'm a non-person whose thoughts are an irrelevance. It was clear that self-determination means nothing to her. But I quickly decided the development was almost certainly to my advantage. I said that I'd be happy to do it. I was now an active member of the meeting, no longer an observer. That gave me strength, and it gave me a new power. Everything was as it should be. The universe was conspiring to facilitate my quest.

Nicholson thanked me for my co-operation, ensuring I had a notepad and pen. He explained that the meeting's purpose was to share information and then to agree on a suitable plan to protect any children who may be vulnerable.

There were two girls in the spotlight. The monster man was an ex-youth worker and paternal grandfather. He had two grandchildren of five and six years, who may be at risk. The girls' parents had been invited to the meeting both orally and in writing but had refused to attend. If the children's names were added to something called the child protection register, the parents would be formally notified. And there'd be a multi-agency child protection plan, which they'd be told about too. It would all be recorded in the minutes I'd be writing. And everyone would get a copy after the chairman signed them as an accurate record, even the parents despite their disinterest. It all seemed reasonably well thought out on first hearing. There's a book of procedures that I've seen since. I think Nicholson wrote it because Maisie said as much. And good for him, I'm sure it's well-intentioned. But I have my own methods of protection. Practises which I know are much more useful than his. I'm sure the multi-agency professionals involved are well-meaning. But they can't guarantee a child's safety as I can. Death is final, and supervision is not.

It seemed the meeting was called a child protection case conference, as opposed to the risk assessment meeting I'd been told of by Maisie. She really should have known that. She has a responsibility. Not that that made much difference to me. I was there to both gather information and develop potential contacts. Whatever the meeting was called, I could do that effectively. And I'd even have written notes of everything that was said. That was a bonus that pleased me. I saw it as a triumph – a big win for me.

The police officer spoke next at Nicholson's request, clearly enunciating his words in a sing-song Welsh accent. He had two metal pips on each shoulder depicting his rank. And I got a distinct impression that he didn't think Simpson should be released at all.

By the time everyone had contributed, I was incredulous. Even by the heinous standards of the monsters I've encountered, Simpson really was a very dangerous man. He doesn't only have the conviction for child rape mentioned by Maisie. As if that wouldn't be bad enough. There was gross indecency too, multiple indecent assaults and even grievous bodily harm. Simpson had been an *extremely* active offender before his arrest, conviction and imprisonment.

The slug had been the enthusiastic leader of a local paedophile ring, with multiple offenders and even more child victims, some still in nappies. He'd used various manipulative methods to silence the many victims, including the use of extreme violence, which he was only too ready to inflict. Children suffered severe physical and psychological injuries. Some survivors were still in therapy years on. Three had ended their lives. Simpson was a hideous man. The word beast could have been invented for him. He was a nonce on steroids, the worst of the worst.

I sat there making hurried scribbled notes while shaking my

head, all the time thinking that the world had gone mad. The fact of Simpson's release seemed an abomination to me. And I could tell some of the others felt the same way. The social worker had said as much in no uncertain terms, voicing her concerns and frustration with the system, bemoaning its many flaws. But her wise words were hot air and no more than that. It was a done deal. Simpson would be back on the streets. Living in the same area in which he'd offended. It was a case of when would he offend again, rather than if. Have you ever heard anything so utterly ridiculous? Why oh why hadn't they thrown away the key?

Nicholson summarised the key points of the meeting once everyone had spoken. The two girls' names were added to the child protection register. And a multi-agency plan of protection was agreed. Simpson would have no contact with the children.

Well, at least, he wouldn't on paper. Whether it worked out that way in the real world may be a different matter. I knew that. I'm sure everyone else at the conference must have known it too.

I once read that the best predictor of future behaviour is past behaviour. That told us all we needed to know. Simpson was what he was. He did what he did. And that hadn't changed. His deviant inclinations hadn't abated. As soon as he got the opportunity, he'd offend again. I've never been more certain of anything in my life.

As we left the conference, I felt even more disillusioned with the system than before. The various professionals were trying their best within the limits of the system. But the risks were still so incredibly high. As we travelled back towards the probation office, I sat mainly in silence. Maisie tried to engage me in conversation more than once as we sped down one road after another, but I had nothing to say. Sometimes mere words are wholly inadequate. And this was one of those occasions.

It was time for action, and I was fully committed. I'd already decided that Simpson was going to die very soon. I've already told you I like to be flexible. He's at the very top of my list now. The scrote's my next target, and he won't die easy. There is any number of tortures for me to inflict. I'm sure you'll agree that he more than deserves it. I may even enjoy it this time. I'll take my time and make him suffer because it pleases me to do so. I'm surprised to be telling you that. It feels different this time.

I'm willing to admit that I appear to be evolving. It seems my behaviour is escalating too.

23

Several days have now passed since that child protection case conference that so disturbed and upset me. All the snow had gone, even the dirty slush at the sides of the roads; all washed away by the winter rain. Simpson has been released from prison on licence. I confirmed that with Maisie, who didn't seem rattled by it at all. It appears that the insanity of the authorities knows no bounds.

I've already tracked my new target down with surprising speed and ease. He's right there on the internet for all to see. It seems he learnt the know-how in prison. He actually did a course which gave him the skills, and all at the taxpayers' expense – a university for the criminal classes. I've heard prison called that. And at least in his case, it's true. It's all there in his file for any member of the probation department who cares to look. It's a scandal. Children should be so much better protected. Are you as surprised as I was when reading his story? I suspect you very probably are.

Simpson is not supposed to have an online presence, but as I've already mentioned, he very obviously has. He's posted several colour photos of a litter of beautiful puppies on a popular social media site. Cute little creatures with black and brown fur that no child could resist. It should be pretty obvious to anyone what the vile beast is up to. And so I created a false profile, something I'm good at, posing as a thirteen-year-old girl this time, the site's minimum age. My fictional bait's a little long in the tooth, given the monster man's past offending pattern. He committed most of his crimes against younger children, the majority under ten years of age. But despite that, I was confident of success if I played my cards right and made no mistakes. The puppy man has been living in a sexual desert, locked up for eight long years with no access to prey. And so I felt sure I could draw him in without too much trouble. He'd take whatever he could get.

It's only a matter of time until the authorities realise what the disgusting bastard's up to. And if they do, Simpson will be recalled to prison to continue his sentence, out of my reach. That is the *last* thing I want. The frustration would be unbearable if he ever escaped me. The very thought is eating away at me right now as I dictate these words. I knew as soon as I found him that I had to act quickly. There was no time for delay. The social media platform offered a simple and convenient way of contacting the monster with a few taps of my keyboard, and so that is precisely what I did.

My first message was a simple one. There was no need for complexity.

Wow, lovely puppies!

That was it, just three words. I felt sure they were more than enough to snag him. And my intuition was spot on. One short sentence was all it took. Simpson got back to me quickly, in a matter of seconds. No surprises there. I would be willing to bet the puppy man was drooling, saliva dripping uncontrollably from his dirty mouth. He didn't comment on my observation.

He just hurriedly directed me to an encrypted message site. Somewhere he could communicate his lies without fear of leaving any evidence that could potentially be used against him. He knew *exactly* what he was doing. Or, at least, he thought he did. Ha! The groomer was being groomed. I liked that. There was a poetry to it, a natural justice that pleased me. It felt as if it was meant to be. Simpson was looking to harm a young teenager, a girl of only thirteen. But instead, I was going to destroy him in the worst possible ways I could think of. I can't undo the tragic past. All the damage he did is done to his many victims. That's a matter of history; it's already written. But I can stop more children being traumatised by this particular monster man and his dark ways. And that's so very worthwhile; such things make my life worth living. I'll take some satisfaction in that.

I shouted out a torrent of crude obscenities as Simpson's first encrypted message appeared on my screen. He'd got straight to it. He really was an *obnoxious cunt*!

Hi there, nice to talk to you, where do you live?

I gave him directions, including the postcode. It's a well-established protocol. Set the trap, hook the monster, and reel the bastard in.

Do you want to see the puppies?

I let out a visceral scream that hurt my throat as it exploded from my mouth.

'I *hate* him. I *fucking well hate him!*'

That summed up my feelings, although no words can

adequately convey the depth of my loathing for this particular beast. Simpson was a man without a conscience, a moral vacuum, a fallen angel from the netherworld. I paced the room, then turned in a circle, gradually calming my breathing, with my hands clenched into tight fists at my sides.

I pictured myself pummelling the puppy man's face to a bloody pulp, and felt a little better. What came next was a crucial part of the process. He was on the hook. I couldn't let him wriggle off. I had to focus, concentrate, handle it well. I couldn't let my hostility get in the way of rational thought. I sat back down on the edge of a chair with my open laptop on the table in front of me and started typing. I told him that I'd *love* to see the puppies, and asked him where I could meet them?

He responded the very second I stopped typing.

Can you come to Tenby?

I unscrewed the metal top from another vodka bottle and took a swig. How I handled his query truly mattered. The uncommonly pleasant Pembrokeshire seaside resort was no good to me at all whatever its attractions. Everything had to happen in *my* territory. He had to come to me to die on my property. That was the only way it was going to work.

I used my usual storyline as I had with Big Boy. I'd be alone, my parents would be away, and the rest. And he took the bait, right there with not even a second's hesitation. I set our meeting up for the following Saturday morning. That gave me more than enough time for planning and preparation. It was going to be a momentous day.

The puppy man said he'd be arriving at 10am sharp. Can you believe that? Sharp! He used that word. As if it was a business appointment rather than a heinous criminal escapade. He'd be leaving his home address at about nine together with the puppies. Oh, and I could keep one too if I wanted one. He even told me to think of a name for the cute little animal. I thought I'd call his imaginary pet Pain because that's what *he'd* suffer. The scrote was in a hurry. He really was a devil. I was looking forward to digging his grave.

24

I visited my mother and sister yesterday evening. Or at least, that was my intention. As it turned out, my sister wasn't in. It was my first visit for... well, let's just say a very long time. I hadn't seen my mother since she gifted me the deposit for the cottage. And my younger sister for even longer than that. I'm not proud of that fact. It fills me with shame. But I hope you can understand that it's hard for me to visit that house so full of bad memories. In a perfect world, I'd never see the place again. And, at the end of the day, neither my mother nor sister have visited me either, now that I think about it.

They've never been anywhere near my cottage, not even once. My maternal grandmother came twice despite my reticence. She said she'd always be there for me if I ever needed her, before she left that second time. And I think she meant it too. But no other family member visited. So maybe the distance I've maintained wasn't such a bad thing after all. It seems we're all trying to forget.

My feelings had changed at least for the moment. Suddenly, I felt I had no choice but to see them, and particularly my mother. I felt driven as I approached that oh-so familiar front door. I'd thought for some days that the events of my life were coming to a head in some strange way. Nothing specific had happened, not really, nothing I could put my finger on. Maybe my drinking had played a part. But either way, I felt as if I was losing control. I'd been having nightmares of my childhood again. And I think maybe it was that rather than the alcohol which had so unnerved me. I hoped my visit might provide some closure, as our American friends like to say. Maybe then I'd find the peace I so crave.

Despite all that, a part of me hoped I wouldn't receive an answer as I knocked on the door. Perhaps it was best to drive the past from my mind. But just as I was about to leave, I saw my mother's silhouette walking down the hall towards me. She opened the door, welcoming me with an unconvincing smile, following which we hugged each other with no warmth at all.

'It's good to see you again, Alice. It's been a while.'

I followed her down the familiar hallway towards the kitchen, memories of the past closing in and threatening. She offered me tea, but I asked for coffee as I sat myself down at the table. The room hadn't changed, and neither had she. Talking to my mother was like trying to get blood from a stone.

'Your sister is at a friend's house.'

I acknowledged her statement with genuine regret. 'Oh, that's a shame, I'm sorry I've missed her.'

'Are you going to have something to eat? You're looking thin. You haven't been looking after yourself properly.'

I shook my head. 'I'm not hungry.'

'Just have a piece of toast.'

'Oh, okay, go on then.' Anything to shut her up.

Mother put two slices of white bread in the toaster. 'How is work?'

'Um, yeah, it's going pretty well, all considered. I'm thinking of training as a probation officer.'

She responded, still standing at the work surface with her back to me. As if she couldn't bring herself to meet my gaze. 'I'd have thought you'd have had enough of criminals, what with your father. Why not do something completely different? Something that makes you happy. Something that could help you forget the past.'

I think my mouth fell open, although I can't be sure. For the first time in my life, my mother had said something meaningful, something brutally honest that almost floored me. Maybe my visit was meant to be.

'Where did that come from?'

She told me she was ill. That there was nothing that the doctors could do. And that my sister would live with her maternal grandmother when the time came.

I asked. 'How long?'

She said, 'Six months at most.'

And I started to cry. I wiped away my tears. 'I killed him, you know, Father, I pushed him off that cliff. It was no accident; it was me.'

She turned to face me now, the toast ready but still warming in the toaster. She thanked me for telling her and said she'd known all along.

'You knew?'

'Yes, yes, I did.'

My eyes narrowed. 'Then, why didn't you say something?'

She hugged me again but with genuine warmth this time. 'I didn't want to risk you being caught. If I'd started talking maybe I couldn't have stopped. I may have blurted something out to the wrong person. I always thought you did the right thing.'

'Really?'

'Oh, yes! I hated that man. I wish I'd dared to do it myself.'

I scratched my nose, asking myself if I should say more. 'Have you... er... have you heard about the recent killing? That paedophile whose car was found on the beach. It's been all over the news.'

She turned away now, back in apparent denial, and I knew I'd said enough.

'What are you going to have on your toast? I've got some lovely, sweet blackberry jam if you fancy it. It's nice on hot toast.'

'That would be perfect.'

'Is there anyone in your life? Any love interest?'

I shook my head again with a humourless laugh. 'No, I don't think men are for me.'

She smiled. 'What about a nice girlfriend, then? Someone to make you happy.'

I grinned, genuinely touched this time. She did seem to have my best interests at heart despite my past thoughts to the contrary. 'No, I don't think that's for me either. I'm quite happy on my own thank you very much.'

'What about children?'

'Not in this life, I couldn't bear it. Maybe in a parallel universe where men like Father don't exist.'

We ate toast and drank our hot drinks together for the next ten minutes or so in virtual silence. She stood when the clock on the wall struck six. 'I need to rest, love. It's been lovely seeing you.'

I kissed her cheek and said I forgave her.

She said, 'Thank you, that means a lot.'

I turned away to leave as she stood there, weeping. As I walked towards my car, I knew a chapter of my life had closed forever. I'd never see my mother again.

25

Another weekend arrived with me alone in my remote stone cottage. The self-inflicted isolation of my existence can be hard to take at times. I'm always alone, even in the company of others. I can't reveal the real me, not my true self, not for a moment. I suffer from a fear of fear, the very feeling of it. The fear of my activities being discovered while there are still monsters in the world to catch and destroy. That burden can be onerous at times. It has a significant negative effect on my life.

I sometimes sit in front of a full-length mirror, eating a meal seated on my slaughterhouse floor. I do it because no one else can be relied on. There's just me and my reflection, my only real friend. I've given that reflection a pet name, but I have no intention of sharing it. She's the only thing I want to keep to myself. She's the only company I can truly trust. Other than my guests, of course. They're the exception to the rule. They come but can never leave. And that gives me solace. I know they can never speak out to betray me like the living.

And so it was time to entertain another gentleman caller. Time to enjoy his company awhile. To introduce him to the dark demons of hell.

I sat in my bedroom thinking the wait was nearly over. He'd soon be arriving, the beast with the fictional puppies in tow. I was prepared; I had everything ready. And I do mean *everything*, even a new blow torch that I'd ordered online. I looked forward to welcoming the beast in my unique way. And I'd enjoy it this time given the extremes of his abusive behaviour. The shock on his face, his denial, his pleading, and his ultimate acceptance. He'd be begging for death in the end, that hurter of children. I was determined to make the bastard suffer. It's what he deserved – the price he had to pay.

I checked my watch for the fourth time that morning. He'd be on his way now, only ten minutes away. I had no doubt he'd be feeling excited but nervous, full of anticipation, his vile obsessions driving his actions, his fantasy-fuelled crimes at the forefront of his mind. I could *not wait* for his arrival. This one *really* mattered to me. It felt totally and utterly personal. I think he may well be the worst abuser I've ever entertained, the king of the monsters, the lord of the flies, a supreme spirit of evil, a plague of misery living amongst us. So, I thought, *Come on, beast, travel to my door. Don't delay. My slaughterhouse is awaiting you, and I'm waiting too.*

I watched through that same bedroom window, asking myself how much suffering a monster man could possibly endure before he finally broke down in mind and spirit. I so wanted him in a miserable state of total mental free-fall before death. I wanted him begging me to kill him. To bring his unhappy existence to a welcome end. It would be more fun for me that way. More entertaining, more rewarding as he faced true justice for the very first time. But how long would it take before he breathed his last breath? How much agony could he endure before his heart gave out? Well, I guess, at the end of the day, that depended on what I did to him. I could cut him but not fatally, break his bones, smash them with my hammer. Oh, and I could burn him too, or peel off his skin. Maybe I should sprinkle a little sea salt on his wounds. That would sting a bit and make the puppy man wince.

There was any number of options I could happily consider. My choices were almost limitless. I remember once reviving a guest when he was very close to death, raising his spirits and then killing him all over again. That was inspired, an act of creative genius. I'm so very proud of those moments when I'm performing at my very best. I gave the monster hope and then snatched it away just when he thought he was going to live to see another day.

I seriously considered following a similar protocol with the puppy man, although I always like to retain some flexibility. I find it works better that way. There's only one way to determine which forms of punishment work best with any particular offender. Up the pressure, turn the screw and see where it gets me. And that's what I resolved to do – after a quick swig of vodka and then maybe another. Yes, another drink or two and I'd be ready to go.

I heard a revving engine as the puppy man sped down my stone track a lot faster than expected about five minutes later. The beast skidded to a sudden halt as he hit the brakes on reaching my yard. He parked next to the pigsty before exiting the car stiffly with a fixed grin on his pasty, sun-deprived face. I turned away from the window and ran for the slaughterhouse, leaping down the stairs two steps at a time. Now all I had to do was lure him into the killing room. The room was dark. My mannequin would distract him. He'd be at my mercy. How hard could it possibly be?

Simpson knocked on the front door only once before pushing it open and entering the hall. That surprised me. He seemed a very different proposition to Big Boy, more confident, more full of himself, wiry and in shape despite his age. He walked down the hallway without speaking before stopping at the base of the stairs. I studied him closely as he stood there. I was looking for weaknesses, any sign of nerves, but he seemed assured. There were no weaknesses to see. He tilted his head to one side, his face expressionless, and then he called out one single word in a rasping, hoarse smoker's voice that filled my cottage with sound.

'Hello!'

That one word seemed to echo in my head. It vibrated off the walls. I do realise that it doesn't make a great deal of sense for me to say that. But that's how it seemed to me at the time. Simpson was very different from any of my previous guests. Something about his bearing told me he was going to be a fighter. This was my Armageddon, a battle between good and evil. And I have to admit that I was feeling far from confident as he sauntered up to my slaughterhouse door.

I very nearly didn't summon him at all as I stood hidden in my nook. A part of me hoped he'd turn away and leave, but only a part of me. I knew it was now or never. Whatever my misgivings, whatever the dangers, I had to stop him. I couldn't let the bastard win. I began tapping my computer keyboard, but my fingers failed to work as if I was losing control of my hands. Stress can do that, I know that now, but it shook me at the time. I resorted to calling out my welcome but my words stuck in my throat, not wanting to escape. But at the second attempt, I succeeded. There was no going back now. It was far too late for that.

'I'm in here, and I'm waiting for you.'

He smiled sardonically as if mocking my very existence. 'Oh, so you're waiting, you little tart.'

And then the beast strode into my slaughterhouse without another word. By the time I crept out of my hiding place, ever so slowly, ever so carefully, cursing the sound of my bare feet on the plastic, he'd already found the light switch. He laughed as he flicked the switch and turned to face me, head back, Adam's apple bobbing, dark mercury fillings in full view. For a fraction of a second, I considered running for the hall and the front door beyond it. But I looked down at the knife held tightly in my hand, and I knew I had to use it. I was the only obstacle between the beast and my butchers' tools, laid out on the floor behind me. Either I was going to use them on him, or he was going to use them against me. And he had the look of a sadist. I really had to act.

I was wishing I hadn't drunk quite so much alcohol as I began swaying ever so slightly to and fro. But I had to strike first however unbalanced. He was taller than me, more muscular and no less determined. A surprise attack was the only advantage I had left.

The monster man glared at me, dressed in my overalls, at the knife in my hand, and then at the butchers' tools behind me.

'Oh, you have made a *big* mistake, love. I eat little girls like you for breakfast. I bet you've got a tight little body underneath those overalls. Why don't you take them off and drop that pathetic knife of yours before I slit your fucking throat with it?'

I gritted my teeth, holding my ground. 'Aren't I a bit old for a filthy nonce like you?'

He took a step towards me, laughing. 'Ah, right, that's what this shit is all about. You're one of those sad little victims. Always whingeing, always moaning, you're *pathetic*. This is a dog-eat-dog world, love. Only the strong survive, and that's not you. I'm going to gobble you up. What part of that don't you understand? You're a fucking snowflake.'

I let him take one final step towards me before hurling myself forward, attempting to strike him with the blade. But he moved quickly, dodging to one side and punching out, landing a heavy blow to my mouth, splitting my lip.

The beast laughed again, coldly, calmly as he weaved from one side to another, his hands raised as fists, preparing to strike again. 'You'll have to do one hell of a lot better than that, love. I learnt to fight in prison. I was in there with some right hard cases. You've got no idea who you're dealing with.'

I spat a tooth to the floor and then lunged at him again, the knife held in front of me. I pulled it back and then thrust it out with all the force I could generate, landing a glancing blow to his left hand as he attempted to parry my attack. The blade sliced his palm, cutting the flesh, inflicting a two-inch wound. He lifted his palm to his mouth, licking it as dark blood dripped down his chin and to the plastic-covered floor. I could see the rage in his eyes as he screwed up his face. A feral growl emitted from his mouth. He was taking on the shape of a beast right there in front of my eyes.

I was panting hard now as I reached down to pick up my hammer, holding it in my right hand with the knife still clutched in my left. I was shaking, but the sight of the monster's blood encouraged me. I was careful to protect my butchers' tools as we mirrored each other in a deadly dance. He tried to dodge past me, and then it happened. Just as I was tiring to the point of exhaustion, the puppy man slipped in his blood. He somehow managed to stay on his feet, but his stumble gave me the opportunity I needed while he was still off-balance. I lifted the hammer high above my head, bringing it crashing down with all my strength, striking him a heavy blow to the left side of his skull a couple of inches above his ear. The beast staggered backwards like a drunken sailor, and then both his legs suddenly gave way as a stream of blood ran from his head wound, soaking into his jumper and shirt.

It was so very tempting to hit him again, to rain down blow after heavy blow until his skull was shattered and his brain revealed. But I held myself back. I'm still so very proud of that. I wanted him dead but not quite yet. There was any number of horrors I was keen to inflict before he took his final breath. But I was hungry; I was thirsty, and I was wearied. I hurried to the bathroom, fetched what was left of my sleeping draught, returning to the monster's side before forcing his mouth open and pouring around five times the prescribed adult dose down his throat. The beast would sleep, and I would rest. I was going to need all my energy for what came next.

26

The puppy man woke up on my slaughterhouse floor at around five the next morning, handcuffed to a black-painted, cast-iron Victorian radiator, which I'd turned off, together with the rest of the heating. The beast tried to yell out when I threw a bucket of cold water in his face, but he couldn't say anything. There were just garbled sounds which made no sense at all. I'd forced a medium-sized orange into his open mouth after drugging him the previous day, and secured it with long lengths of strong yellow tape wrapped around his head, which was now swollen but no longer bleeding.

He'd no doubt try to scream as my plans for him materialised. That was as inevitable as night and day. But I was in no rush to hear him. I would remove his gag at some point. He would have his opportunity to plead his case, but not quite yet. There would be plenty of time for that.

I'd cut off all the beast's clothes while he slept, and so he was naked, cold and shivering. I'd already moved his car. And I'd placed a broom handle between his legs, from his groin to his ankles, wrapping a large quantity of tape around his legs for their entire length. I'd be safer that way. I'd be able to work without fear of him kicking out. And there'd be other advantages too. I was confident my preparations would make him feel more vulnerable, increasing his distress. And it gave me better access to his body. He couldn't curl up, raising his knees to his chest, which would make the entire process easier for me. I had considered inserting the broom handle into his rectum for several inches. But the angles weren't right, and so I abandoned the idea, such a shame.

All my butchers' tools were still laid out on the slaughterhouse floor a short distance from the beast's bare feet. I could see him looking at them as I threw the bucket to one side, bouncing it off the nearest wall for the fun of it. His eyes burned red as he began throwing himself about, twisting first one way and then another, tugging violently at his handcuffs, but with little, if any hope of success. I think he may have had a premonition of what was to come because he pissed himself. It was my turn to laugh now as yellow urine soaked his lower body, and the steel handcuffs cut into the skin of his wrists. I stood there in front of him, watching as he continued struggling, right up to the time he slowed and eventually stopped. He'd given in, and I found some satisfaction in that.

I dropped to my knees a few feet in front of him, staring into his tear-filled eyes. 'Oh, no, now you've gone and soiled yourself. Maybe I should have bought you some nappies. Are you ready for some fun, nonce? Your worst nightmare is about to come true.'

He was whining now, like one of those imaginary dogs of his. Oh, the irony!

'You should have stayed in prison when you had the chance. You could con the idiot authorities, but you can't con me. I know *exactly* what you are, you piece of filth. You're the disease, and I'm the cure. Buckle up, Mr Puppy Man. This is going to be the worst day of your sad life. Prepare for a bumpy ride.'

The beast began rocking violently, attempting to pull the radiator from the wall. But things were made to last in those long-gone days. His efforts were wasted. He made no impact at all.

I rose quickly to my feet, stood over him, drew my arm back and slapped his face hard with an open hand. 'Shut the fuck up! I'm in control here. I can do whatever the hell I want. And don't go thinking you can escape me. False hope is no hope. Others have tried and failed. You're going to die as they did. But we'll have some fun together before then. I want you to nod once if you understand.'

He pressed himself against the radiator as if trying to disappear into the wall. But he didn't nod. I picked up my utility knife, gripped his head with one arm, holding it in place, and then I sliced off the tip of his nose. He wailed as blood poured from his wound, soiling both of us in red. I released his head, taking a backward step to admire my work.

'When I give you an instruction, you follow it. What part of that don't *you* get? Maybe now you understand how your victims felt – all those little children who encountered a beast. I've got all the power now, and you'll do what *I* say. If you don't, I'll cut something else off. It is that simple: a finger maybe, or a toe, or that tiny little dick of yours. You've done a lot of damage with that thing, but you're not going to need it anymore. Nod once if you understand.'

This time he nodded.

'Very well done, Mr Puppy Man, now we're getting somewhere. I think at last you're starting to comprehend your predicament. Give me a minute; I need a bit of breakfast before we continue. But don't you worry, I'll be back with you soon enough, and then we'll start your trial. You'll be found guilty of course, that's a given. But it's only fair to allow you to have your say. I may even remove your gag for that. You can plead your case, make your lame excuses. And then I'll decide on your punishment. You may be able to influence how much you suffer. I may even show you mercy, but probably not. It's not as if you showed any to those little ones you treated so very badly. Things have gone full circle, Simpson. You're the victim now. This is it, your time to pay.'

And with that said, I turned away to leave the room. I wasn't in the mood to eat, but a strong, sweet coffee was very welcome. I was tempted to add a tot of whisky to the aromatic blend but decided against it– something I found more difficult than it sounds. I felt refreshed and alert when I returned to my slaughterhouse, where I found the beast weeping, his face a bloody mess. Not a pretty sight, but it pleased me nonetheless. I stood immediately in front of my captive noting everything about him. I cleared my throat and spat in his face before speaking.

'Tell me how many children you abused before being caught and imprisoned. Nod once if it was more than ten, twice if it was more than twenty, and so on. And remember, I've read your probation file. I know the sort of vile things you were involved with. Lie even once, and I'll punish you. Make no mistake. This is a time for the truth.'

The beast didn't move an inch. He sat there glaring up at me with his hands cuffed behind him. I could smell his fear. The room reeked of it. His lack of response left me physically shaking as I picked up my hammer. I lifted it high above my head, bringing it crashing down on his left kneecap. He recoiled with a guttural groan as I repeated the process on his right leg.

'I'm going to ask you again. How many?'

He nodded now, but only once.

I picked up the blow torch next, lighting it and burning his bare chest for a minute or two as his whimpering became an agonised wail. There was a smell of charred meat that stimulated my appetite. I stopped when he was close to passing out. I didn't want that. I needed him awake.

'How many?'

The beast nodded three times.

I paced the room, attempting to cope with the emotional impact of his statement. I needed a drink. Thirty children was terrible; no, that's an understatement. It was horrendous. But I was sure he was still minimising his guilt. They always do that. There had very probably been more. I relit the blow torch, burning all the hair from his head. The scalp was left red and blistered.

'I want the truth, nothing but the truth. This is your *final* opportunity to come clean. Confession is good for the soul.'

The puppy man nodded slowly, a total of five times.

I screamed now and then ran for the vodka bottle. I gulped down my fill before approaching him again.

'*Fifty! Fucking fifty!* You're a plague, a virus. What the fuck is wrong with you? You're the scum of the earth.'

He looked away for the first time, averting his eyes to the door. That amused me. He wanted to be anywhere else but there. I picked up my utility knife from the floor, holding it in clear sight.

'Fifty cuts for fifty victims, that's my kind of justice. Now, where shall I start?'

I sat facing him, straddling his legs close to his shattered kneecaps and began slicing his flesh, all over his upper body, each cut approximately an inch long and two to three inches apart. Soon the entire area became a sea of red as the blood ran from his wounds. I'd just reached the total number of cuts commensurate with that part of his sentence when I realised he was barely conscious. His chin had fallen to his chest. I had to act quickly. I ripped what was left of the partially molten plastic tape from his head and removed the orange from his mouth, something I could only achieve by extracting four of his front teeth with pliers.

I stood back, looking at him, planning the final stage of his trial and punishment. He was almost unrecognisable as the monster man who'd arrived at my home so full of lousy intention the previous day.

I felt satisfied with what I'd achieved up to that point. But it wasn't finished. There was more to come. He'd suffered, but not nearly enough. Another bucket of cold water and the beast was awake again; not wide awake, but hanging on in there, clinging onto his miserable life as if it mattered. As if it was worth something.

'Do you feel any remorse for what you've done? I'm interested. Really, I want to know.'

I struggled to understand his reply. His mouth opened, but his words were garbled. I placed my face close to his, repeating the same question, louder this time.

He tried again, attempting to speak slowly, to force the words from his mouth. I got the general gist but no more than that. He was trying to tell me to kill him. He wanted it over. I sliced off his right ear. Death would come, but not quite yet.

'Are you sorry for your crimes? You should be. You've damaged a lot of innocent lives.'

He raised his head momentarily, mouthed the words fuck off, and then dropped his chin again. I cut off his other ear, throwing it to the floor behind me, close to the door. When the beast attempted to spit at me, I couldn't take anymore. I picked up my utility knife to cut his throat. He bled out in seconds. He won't be hurting any more children. That, I can guarantee you. Now it was over; child protection at its most influential and decisive. I'd done my bit, and I'm proud of that.

27

Dismembering the puppy man's wiry corpse was less onerous than Big Boy's, but it was still demanding, which was no surprise at all. I didn't have to deal with the mounds of flabby flesh but sawing through the beast's sinew, ligaments and bone was taxing, especially after the effort involved with his trial and eventual execution. Over two hours had passed by the time I finished dissecting the body. My mouth was on fire, and I was aching. I drank almost a quarter of a vodka bottle to dull the pain but with only limited success. I was so drained that I started crying. Even my usual musical accompaniment didn't raise my flagging spirits. I couldn't bring myself to dance at all.

I began bagging the body parts after a light lunch which was challenging to eat. My traumatised gum was still causing me a good deal of pain despite two analgesic tablets washed down with alcohol. I used a newly acquired metal wheelbarrow to transport the limbs, torso and head to my rose garden at the back of the cottage. It was easier that way. I'd learnt from experience. I'd decided to create a second flower bed. And so the digging served a dual purpose. Firstly to hide the evidence from a misguided world, and secondly to create a scented oasis I could enjoy in the warmer months. I plan to plant new roses in the spring, which will gain nourishment from the puppy man's decomposing flesh and organs. I've decided that pink blooms would best complement the yellow flowers already planted. It's going to be stunning. I'll look forward to that.

The ground was soft but saturated after the recent thaw. The digging was more challenging than expected, as puddles of muddy water formed in the hole within seconds of me bailing it out. I had intended to dig down five or six feet or so. But I soon realised that such a depth wasn't realistic given the conditions. I've already explained that I like to be flexible. And so I decided on three feet. Even that wasn't easy. It had started to rain again by the time I dropped the beast's final body part into his grave. I quickly shovelled in the earth, stamping it down as necessary in a finishing flourish.

I was cold, dirty and shivering as I walked back towards my cottage to clean up my slaughterhouse and tools. They serve me well and warrant looking after. I think that's the least I can do.

A long hot shower, a change of clothing, and I was ready to get rid of the car a few hours later. I waited until after dark, of course. And I planned to avoid that same beach resort for fear of being seen. But there's always an alternative if you think about it hard enough. I settled on a local woodland about five miles from my home. The car was old, an unreliable rust bucket. But it somehow kept going until I was deep in the forest in the early hours of the morning. I took a red metal petrol can, usually used for my lawnmower, from the boot, soaked both the inside and outside of the car with the flammable liquid, and set it alight with the toss of a match. I so felt like a drink as I watched the flames leap and dance for a few seconds, surprised by the burning intensity of inferno. Dark smoke spiralled into the night-time air, and then the petrol tank exploded, a shock wave of energy knocking me off my feet and onto my back.

I struggled upright with a pained frown, keen to get out of there as quickly as possible as the forest came alive. Could life get any better? Yes, it fucking well could. I turned away without looking back and cursed crudely under my breath. If my father were watching, he'd be laughing. It was time to get away. Some things never change. It was going to be another long walk home.

28

I took a few days sick leave after the puppy man's visit and
eventual departure, having told Maisie a close relative had
died unexpectedly at a regrettably young age. I wouldn't say I
liked lying, not about something like that. It didn't make me feel
good about myself. But it was something I had to do. A relatively
minor sin to support the bigger picture, that's the way I look at it.
In reality, I needed time to recover. Time to let my injuries heal.
My split lip was still slightly swollen but healing. There was a
little scab, but it was hardly noticeable. But my missing tooth
was a lot harder to ignore. The glaring gap in my front teeth
made me cringe every time I looked in the bathroom mirror.
The light is so very bright, and so I couldn't miss it. But as
shaken as I was, I still didn't feel that either injury justified any
more time off work. I was feeling guilty about being paid to do
nothing. And hanging around the cottage resulted in more
drinking.

So I applied more make-up than usual to mask my
remaining bruising, got into my car, and drove to the probation
office to get on with my life. I played a favourite country music
CD as I went and sang along to the familiar tunes. I wasn't

planning another killing for a week or two. It was time to concentrate on my career, and I needed time to regain my strength.

I parked in my usual spot, checked my make-up in the car's vanity mirror for one final time, and exited the vehicle, intending to act as if I hadn't been away. I was very much hoping that my colleagues would ignore my facial flaws, saying nothing at all. But it didn't work out that way, not even close. Maisie studied my face as soon as she saw me. She made polite conversation initially asking me how the fictional funeral went, but I could see her staring at me. I knew a question was coming. I could feel it in my bones.

'Alice, I've got to ask. What on earth happened to your face?'

I silently admonished myself for not having prepared an adequate explanation in advance. Something to shut the interfering bitch up. My chest tightened. It wasn't like me to be so ill-prepared. *Think, Alice, think.* 'I, er, I slipped on the ice.'

'Oh dear, when?'

I took a backward step as my head began to ache. The bitch seemed suspicious. Why was she still asking questions? 'It happened at the funeral.'

Maisie appeared less than persuaded. Why oh why was she sticking her nose in? How dare she? What the hell?

'But I thought most of the snow had gone by then? How on earth did it happen?'

The nosey bitch was saying too much and asking too much also. Such a big mouth. I tapped my foot against the floor. *Shut up, Maisie, shut up, shut up, shut the fuck up!* I wanted to say it. I wanted to shout it. To grip her shoulders to shake her until she learnt the error of her ways. But I somehow kept control.

'The funeral was in Scotland. It's colder there.'

'Scotland? You didn't mention it.'

I clenched my hands, digging the nails into my palms before

relaxing my fingers. What the hell was wrong with the woman? Why another question? Always more questions. I had thought she liked me, that she wanted to be my friend. So much had changed. My control was slipping now. I needed a drink. I wanted to slap her, to silence her, to tape her mouth shut. That evening in the Indian restaurant now felt so very long ago.

'My cousin lived near Edinburgh. I flew up from Cardiff. I thought I told you.' I was pleased with my quick thinking. I thought I'd done well under pressure. I still do. But even that wasn't enough to shut the bitch up. Maisie smiled as she suggested a coffee. But I knew what she was up to. She was trying to catch me out. You can't kid a kidder. I'd played that game before.

'I'll put the kettle on.'

Maisie followed me as I headed to the staff kitchen. Can you believe that? The sneaky, meddlesome bitch! She wouldn't leave me alone, even for a moment. Maybe going back to work was a mistake after all.

'You must have had one hell of a fall to knock out a tooth, poor you. Have you made a dental appointment?'

'No, not as yet, I haven't had the time.'

She pulled her lips back, revealing those over-white teeth of hers. As if they were something I wanted to see. 'I can highly recommend my guy if you're interested. He's a bit pricey, but he's worth it.'

I'd been trying to talk without revealing my teeth. But now she knew. She'd made that clear with her snide comments. And she was asking those invasive questions again, pretending she wanted to help. Just to annoy me, to increase my discomfort. I hated her for that. I filled the kettle and switched it on, willing her to leave the room.

'I'm happy with my dentist, thanks.'

She smiled again, revealing those gleaming teeth as if

mocking my misfortune. Did she know what had really happened? Was that what she was getting at? Did she know Simpson was dead?

'Okay, if you're sure. But he really is *excellent*. Let me know if you change your mind.'

My hand was shaking as I spooned instant coffee granules into two mugs. Maisie had her hand on the door handle now. Thank God for small mercies. She was about to go. That would at least give me time to think.

'I'll see you in my office, Alice. No biscuits for me today, thanks. I'm on a diet. I'm starting to look like a beached whale.'

I poured the boiling water, vapour rising in the air. Why had she said such a thing? Was she playing me as I had her? Yes, that was it; she was trying to draw me in with her feigned friendship. She was encouraging me to talk openly, to share my many secrets. And then, of course, she'd betray me, my Judas. But I was never going to let that happen. Does she think I'm that stupid? Maisie's not to be trusted. She's a snake in the grass.

'You look fine to me.'

She opened the door, raising my hopes. 'I don't think Rob would agree with you.'

Why mention her piggy police husband? Was it some veiled threat? What if she pointed the police in my direction? Perhaps I should kill her too.

'I'll bring you your coffee when it's ready.'

Maisie nodded and then finally left. No doubt preparing for her next verbal attack.

As I delivered Maisie's hot beverage to her office a minute later, I was planning to place it on her desk, and then get out of there as fast as possible. The last thing I wanted was another interrogation. But once again, she was there with her questions. She seemed obsessed with my life. Why oh why didn't she ever shut up? She just wouldn't let it go.

'Thanks, Alice, much appreciated as always. It's good to have you back.'

I went to leave. But she wouldn't let me slip away. 'Aren't you going to sit down for a chat?'

I felt like screaming. 'I've got work to catch up with.'

'Oh, come on, you can spare five minutes, there's something I want to tell you.'

I pictured her gagged and bleeding, handcuffed in my cottage like those before her. I met her eyes, but I didn't sit. I looked at my watch, making it obvious. 'What is it?'

'Simpson's missing, the offender we discussed at the meeting. The police aren't jumping to any conclusions. But Rob says they suspect it may be murder.'

My entire body was trembling. 'Is DI Kesey involved?'

'She's the senior investigating officer. She's heading up a major investigation team.'

Oh God, they were looking for me. They were getting closer. The room became an impressionist blur as I dropped my coffee to the floor. I could hear Maisie saying something, but she sounded so far away, somewhere in the distance. And then my legs gave way under me and down I went. Everything went black as I hit the carpet.

29

I came around on Maisie's office floor with a green uniformed paramedic I recognised from school looming over me, larger than life and twice as ugly. His younger female colleague stood behind him, holding some kind of stretcher with a stupid smirk on her pixy face. Maisie was in her usual seat looking down at me, still snooping in that sneaky way of hers, no surprises there. But at least it wasn't the police. I wasn't being arrested, or, at least, not yet. Maybe things weren't quite as bad as I'd first feared. The older of the two paramedics was the first to speak.

'Hi, Alice, nice to have you back with us. I think you must have fainted. My name is David Williams. Call me Dai. Do you remember me from school? I was in the upper sixth when you were in the lower.'

My head hurt when I tried to raise it. I said I remembered him very well.

'Right, stay where you are. Don't try to get up. You've had a bit of a bang on the head. You hit the corner of the desk on your way down. I've patched you up as best I can, but you're going to need a couple of stitches when we get you to the hospital. Is there anything I need to know about? Diabetes, epilepsy, anything along those lines?'

'I've been under a *lot* of stress.'

'Ah, right, that makes sense. We'll tell the doctors all about it. Now, try your best to relax. You're in good hands. You're going to be okay.'

I repeatedly blinked, attempting to clear my vision. There were tiny stars everywhere I looked. 'I think, I think I'm going to puke.'

He turned me on my side as the female I didn't know hurriedly left the room. She returned less than a minute later with a cardboard receptacle, which she placed on the floor close to my face. I held it to my mouth, spitting out a mouthful of vomit.

'Are the police coming?'

Dai took my hand in his, looking down at me with a puzzled expression. 'Why would the police be coming?'

I closed my eyes, unable to come up with an answer. I wondered if he was lying. Perhaps he was conning me. Maybe the three of them were in it together. However, there were no blue lights. And I hadn't heard a siren.

'What happened to your mouth?'

Oh, for fuck's sake! Now he was snooping too. Was there *anyone* I could trust? Why did everyone feel the need to stick their noses into my private affairs?

'I slipped on the ice.'

'What, onto your face?'

I snapped back at him. 'Nobody hit me if that's what you're thinking. Not that it's any of your business.'

He turned and nodded towards his colleague. No one believed a word I said. I could sense the tension. It was written all over their faces.

'Okay, let's get her onto the stretcher.'

The younger paramedic stepped forward with a broad smile I didn't appreciate. She spoke with a local accent, but I hadn't seen her before that day. I think she's a snooper too.

'We're going to get you checked out at the hospital, Alice. Don't you worry. We'll look after you. You relax, we'll do the lifting.'

I wanted to jump up, to run and keep running, but there was nowhere to go. And my head hurt so very badly. My vision still hadn't cleared. Maybe I was suffering from concussion. I heard someone mention the word at some point. I'm not sure who. I let them roll me onto the stretcher. I had no fight left.

Maisie followed as the two paramedics carried me towards the ambulance at the far side of the small car park. The bitch still wouldn't allow me a moment's peace. She still wouldn't shut the fuck up. What the hell is wrong with the woman? She's become another dark shadow pulling me down, a watcher brimming with bad intentions.

'I don't want you back in work until you're well, Alice. Do you hear me? You need a good long rest. I'm speaking as your boss now as well as your friend. You haven't been yourself lately. I'll give you a ring sometime tomorrow to see how you're doing. I've got your mobile number. *Please* do whatever the doctors tell you to do. You need to look after yourself.'

At that very moment, my father appeared, laughing like a demented hyena, no doubt due to Maisie's lecture. The bastard chooses his times so very well. He always makes an appearance when I'm at my most vulnerable. How does he do that? I couldn't see him, but he was there. Chatter, chatter, chatter. I could hear him whispering in my ear.

She's onto you, Alice. She knows your secrets. It's only a matter of time till you're caught.

Father taunted me like that time and again, and I feared the others could hear him too. My freedom was hanging by a thread.

I yelled out to silence him. 'Shut the fuck up, you monster. Get out of my life!'

Maisie and the two paramedics were looking at each other now, exchanging knowing glances, as if they thought me insane. No one seemed to understand what was happening except me. Only I knew the truth. That's not a nice place to be, at the centre of a mad world. I clawed at my scalp as Dai closed the vehicle's rear doors with me in the back, strapped to some sort of mattress. He sat alongside me with an open hand resting on my shoulder, pressing down a little too firmly for my liking. The female I didn't know did the driving.

'Don't struggle, Alice. We don't want you falling again, now, do we? The straps are for your own good. Please try your best to relax. Throwing yourself about isn't going to help you at all.'

He plunged a needle deep into my upper arm as I glared up at him screaming. I tried to bite him with a rapid jerk of my head, but he moved quickly, jumping back before my mouth reached his arm. He was the winner and I the loser. I'm sure that amused my father, no end. Within seconds I was drowsy, then unconscious. I was lost to welcome sleep. If only it had stayed that way. Maybe it would have been better if I hadn't woken up at all.

30

I arrived at my GP surgery two days later with a hospital letter in a sealed brown envelope clutched tightly in my right hand. I handed it in to the sour-faced receptionist and then sat for what seemed like an age in the overcrowded waiting room, glancing at one out-of-date magazine after another before eventually taking my phone from my pocket.

I wasn't concerned about my health, not in the slightest. I haven't got any problems to speak of. But seeing my doctor was the only way I was ever going to get back to work. So I sat there and waited like a good little girl, doing what I was told, playing their ridiculous games. At least my visit would provide an opportunity to obtain some more of my sleeping draught. That was a positive. I took some satisfaction in that.

I was finally called to see the doctor about half an hour or so after my arrival. By that time, I'd discarded my reading material and had identified another potential target on my smartphone. They're such useful little devices – mines of helpful information for the curious. As I stood, I consoled myself with the fact that the time waiting hadn't been entirely wasted. I'd sent an invite to my next prospective gentleman caller. He wasn't hooked quite yet. But he soon would be. Another monster man would be on his way. This time I was posing as a sixteen-year-old girl. A little older than usual. But it served my purpose.

Dr Warren sat behind her messy desk looking more concerned than I'd ever seen her before. I assumed her demeanour was something to do with me. We live in a perverse world where the wise are often misunderstood. She had the letter open in front of her. 'Take a seat, Alice. There are things we need to discuss. I've asked my receptionist not to send in another patient for at least fifteen minutes.'

'I'm in a bit of a rush.'

Her expression darkened. 'We can always arrange an alternative appointment if that suits you better.'

I shrugged, accepting defeat, my hands held wide. 'Okay, let's get on with it.'

'You were taken into the hospital directly from your workplace first thing in the morning. And yet your blood tests showed that your blood alcohol level was three times the legal limit for driving. I'm concerned, Alice. Is there anything you want to tell me?'

'They must have mixed my results up with somebody else.'

She frowned hard. 'I very much doubt that was the case.'

'I'm not a drinker. I enjoy an occasional glass of wine, and that's it. I don't know what more I can say.'

She glanced at the letter again and then at me. 'The casualty consultant tells me that you refused to speak to a psychiatrist despite his advice. Can you tell me about that?'

I blew out a series of short breaths. 'I fainted, I had a fall, I'm not mentally ill. Why would I need a psychiatrist?'

The look on her face suggested she was finding the conversation almost as tricky as I was. Why didn't she shut her stupid mouth?

'You appeared to have been hearing voices.'

I asked myself why everyone was against me, even her. *What a bitch!* 'I'd had a bang on the head. I'm fine now. I don't hear voices. I never have. This is becoming ridiculous.'

She sighed. 'If you won't agree to see a psychiatrist I would at least like you to speak to a counsellor. We have an excellent one here at the surgery every Wednesday afternoon.'

I wasn't going to fall into that trap. 'I just want some more sleeping medication. That's the only thing I need. I can't sleep without it. Are you going to help me or not?'

She checked her computer screen. 'You should have *plenty* left according to my records. It's not something you should overuse. It's addictive, and there are some potentially unpleasant side effects. It's not a long-term answer. I really think talking to the counsellor would be a good idea.'

'I dropped the bottle. Most of it was spilt. I wouldn't dream of taking too much.'

She picked up her prescription pad, and I knew I was finally winning. 'How about we make a deal? I'll write you a prescription for the syrup if, and only if, you'll agree to see the counsellor next Wednesday at two. It's a one-hour appointment.'

'What about work?'

She held the nib of her biro above her prescription pad, preparing to write. 'We can talk about that *after* your therapy session but not before.'

I stood as she handed me the prescription, keen to get out of there with no more talk.

'Don't leave quite yet, please, Alice. I'd like to weigh you and take your blood pressure. And it wouldn't be a bad idea to repeat your blood tests. It's just routine. Nothing to worry about.'

I decided to go along with it in the interests of an easy life. I had no intention whatsoever of seeing the counsellor. Why would I need to? I'd make my excuses at the appropriate time. I may well need another prescription at some future date. A little tranquillising medication is always handy. I played the game. It was worth keeping my doctor onside.

31

I 've killed again, another execution, using the same well-established protocol. I've had so much time on my hands due to my enforced sick leave. I was keen not to waste it. And so my quest continues. There was no car to get rid of this time. My gentleman caller came by train. I took a gamble, collecting him from the station at three o'clock one sunny Saturday afternoon. I hope that doesn't come back to haunt me as the weeks pass. Maybe I was unwise to act so instinctively. But I was in a blue funk, bored, and it seemed like too good an opportunity to miss. So, what the hell, I got on with it.

Over a week has now passed since my latest guest's arrival. He's still there dead on my slaughterhouse floor. I can see him lying there on the clear plastic sheeting as I write these words. He's covered in body art, my latest guest, high-quality tattoos from ankles to neck. Ink at its stunning, creative best. Or, at least, I like to think so. And his skin is so very soft, like the best quality leather, although it's deteriorating a little more with each hour that passes. I just can't bring myself to put him in the ground. Not yet, not until I have to. There's so much artwork to see and appreciate while I still can. Perhaps I'll skin the rest of him before it's too late. It will be so very nice to preserve the best of the tattoos as a keepsake.

There was one of a sizeable leaping panther on his back that I particularly liked. I've already removed it with my utility knife. A messy job better done by experts, but I was careful not to damage the image. I think I did a reasonable job of it too. I plan to frame the hide when I get the chance to hang it on my wall for posterity. I've already measured for and ordered a suitable frame. Black ebony wood to match the black panther, with a white cardboard mounting to make it stand out. I paid a premium, but I'm sure it will be worth it. One gets what one pays for in this life of ours. It will be a lovely reminder of the time we spent together chatting in my bone-house – a memento I can treasure until my dying day.

I shared a meal and a bottle of wine with the panther boy yesterday evening, finished off with a French brandy in a crystal glass. I've become rather fond of his company. There was just me, him, my mannequin, the mirror and my reflection, all sat together on my slaughterhouse floor. There wasn't much conversation to speak of, but I appreciated the company. I think of them all as friends now, although I realise the panther boy will soon have to go.

I've kept the room as cool as possible to preserve the body in a reasonable state. But there's only so long that's acceptable as spring fast approaches and the temperature rises. His face is already becoming more of a skull than a person in places. And my lavender air freshener is no longer adequate to alleviate the smell however much I use. I've gone through two full cans already and have had to buy a third.

Soon I'll have to face the inevitable and say my fond farewells. It's such a shame, so very regrettable. I'm going to miss him terribly when he's gone. But I'll still have my memories, no one can take those from me. I'm glad he came at all; I'll focus on the positives. He spent time with me here, my friend and confidante. I'll just have to be grateful for that.

The panther boy was the first of my many guests to express genuine remorse and regret. I think that's to his credit. He was a nineteen-year-old young man with long blond hair and sky-blue eyes, who'd experienced abuse himself, or so he claimed as we talked of times gone by. He sat there naked and beautiful, chained to my black Victorian radiator, and told me that he'd thought the girl was sixteen when he had sex with her months before. She'd told him as much, or so he claimed when the two of them met in a student bar one drunken Friday night in September. That doesn't make it right, of course. It doesn't in any way excuse his crime. That goes without saying. But something about his demeanour told me his claim might well have been true. He was crying when he said it, a torrent of tears rolling down his handsome face as if they may never stop. And they seemed like tears of regret rather than self-pity.

That impressed me; he had empathy for the girl. He wasn't a complete monster like the others. I could have forgiven him if my circumstances had been different. I may even have let him go after a reasonable period of punishment to get on with his life. But, of course, that wasn't possible. Not in this life, not in my world, there's too much at stake.

He promised he wouldn't say anything; that he wouldn't go to the police. He swore it on his mother's life. And he declared that he'd never touch an underage girl again too, even if she looked sixteen and consented as I had in my messages.

But I'm sure you'll understand that was a risk I couldn't afford to take. I spent one final afternoon with my panther boy, chatting, listening to his life story and telling him mine.

I appreciated the opportunity to pour out my angst. I introduced him to my father, who made an inevitable appearance as the alcohol flowed. I described how I killed

Father, pushing him off that cliff, the start of it all. And we discussed my previous guests, which seemed to unnerve the panther boy for some reason I still can't fully comprehend. Maybe it was my description of their offending behaviour that so upset him. Or the extremes to which I went to punish them for their crimes. Although I like to think the boy appreciated my motives. I killed for a good reason. I think he understood that before he died himself.

I shed a tear for the panther boy as I picked up my utility knife, already fitted with a sharp new blade. I didn't want him to suffer as I slowly approached him, kneeling at his side and gently lifting his chin. I could feel him tense as he closed his blue eyes tight shut. And then I cut his throat, quickly from ear to ear, being careful not to damage a tattoo starting at the base of his neck. I dropped the knife to the floor and held the boy's hand as he bled out, offering him comfort as I sang a lullaby into his ear. I think he appreciated that because he died easy. Maybe he was as fond of me as I was of him.

32

Maisie came to visit as I was busy working in my rose garden. Regrettable timing I'm sure you'll agree. I'm sorry if I seem to be making light of it. Because it did unnerve me at the time. She blew my plans right out of the water with one thoughtless act. What the hell is wrong with the woman? Why does she feel the need to interfere in my private affairs as often as she does? I could quite easily scream. But what would that achieve? She's a bitch, I know that much, but as for the rest of it... I'll put it down to the mysteries of life. Maybe you'll let me know if you can come up with an explanation.

I was digging the wet ground when the bitch arrived. I was preparing the panther boy's final resting place with fond love and affection, when I heard the unmistakable sound of a vehicle approaching the cottage, just a few hundred metres away. I thought for one glorious but all too fleeting moment that my ebony picture frame was about to be delivered. But as I rushed around to the front of the building in my green wellingtons, my heart sank as I recognised the flash silver convertible. Maisie! At my home, she was there on my territory, invading my personal space, breathing my air. How dare she? How fucking well dare she? The *bitch*, the total and utter *bitch*!

I swore as I crouched down low out of her sight. And then I retreated, turning and crawling behind a convenient stone wall bordering the lawn, where I could be sure she wouldn't spot me with those snooping eyes of hers. I knew then that she was out to get me. She was poison, a wolf in sheep's clothing. My suspicions had been correct all along. She'd become my nemesis, a virus seeking my downfall. I was determined not to let her win. If she wanted a fight, she was going to have one – the most challenging fight of her life. I'd beaten bigger and harder. She wouldn't find me wanting. I'd gained far too much experience for that.

My hatred for Maisie was so very intense that I thought my skull might crack with the pressure of it all. I cursed her very existence as I headed towards the back door, still out of the bitch's sight. I hurried through the cottage to the lounge at the building's front after locking the back door behind me. I'd never wanted someone to fuck off more as I peeped through the lounge curtains. I called out, telling the panther boy as much, but, of course, he didn't reply. He no longer has a voice. But I know he'd have felt the same were he still able to speak.

My father mocked me as Maisie exited her convertible in a tight floral dress, locking the car door with the click of a button. I chose to ignore him as the bitch pushed open my garden gate and strolled towards my front door in those high-heeled shoes of hers as if she owned the place. And then she knocked on my door as if that was okay. As if it was a reasonable thing to do. The woman is deluded, dangerous, around the fucking bend. I hated her even more for that. She's devoid of any redeeming qualities.

I waited, willing Maisie to walk away, but she kept knocking, harder and louder as the seconds passed by. Then she had the audacity to bend down to peer through my letter box. To look into my hall without my permission; what a dreadful unredeemable bitch. And then, as if that weren't bad enough, she actually pushed the letter box open and called out through it, so loud that I couldn't fail to hear her in my hiding place.

'Hello, Alice, *please* answer the door. I know you're in there. I can see your car. I'm concerned, I've tried to ring you. I have a duty of care as your manager. I need to know you're okay.'

The car, my fucking car! I'd given it no thought at all. Why hadn't I hidden the damned thing? Attention to detail was everything. I felt my remaining confidence slipping away. Why oh why hadn't I thought of it before? I'd let myself down.

I heard my father's all too familiar voice, and this time I saw him again. There he was standing in those jet-black clothes of his with that starched white dog collar around that scrawny neck, picking his moments as he does so very well. He was chipping away at my self-esteem, as is his custom. Why won't my tormentor leave me alone?

You silly girl, you make one stupid mistake after another. You're a screw-up, Alice, my little plaything, a waste of space and breath.

I shook a fist at him while baring my teeth in a snarl that didn't seem to faze him at all. 'I managed to shove you off that cliff without too much trouble, preacher man. I watched you plunge to your death. I did that, *me*! And I got away with it too. I wasn't silly then.'

But look at you now, Alice, crouching there, nervous, trembling, such a sad sight for a father to behold.

'Shut up, Father, or she'll hear you. Get back to hell. Hide under the devil's tail. That's where you belong. You've done enough damage in my life. I detest you and Mother loathes you too. I've got work to do. It's time for you to go.'

Let her in, Alice. You're going to have to talk to her sometime, you ridiculous girl. If she goes away, she'll come back. And she'll bring the police. Where will your little escapade be then, my girl? Let the woman in. It's the only choice you've got.

I crouched there, still hidden, considering my limited options in light of my father's unwelcome input. I tugged at my hair on asking myself if he were correct for the very first time. But I dismissed the idea as laughable as I reached for a vodka bottle. What the hell was I thinking? He was toying with me for his amusement, to do me down, as he always had. He was a monster when I was a child, and he's a monster still. It would be crazy to even listen to the bastard, let alone do what he said.

I let out a silent cheer as Maisie knocked on my door for one last time before walking back down my path towards my gate. But my joy proved premature when a minute or two later she tried to open the door at the rear of the cottage. And then, as if that wasn't enough of an intrusion, she began looking through the ground-floor windows one at a time, prying into my private world, her tarty face pressed against the glass. I scuttled from one room to another on all fours, ensuring I was not seen as I continued to watch her. Thankfully, the slaughterhouse curtains were closed. That was fortunate. I think that may well have saved me. Had she seen it she'd have run, called the police, the game would have been up. But the panther boy remained my special secret. I thought to wait it out. To ignore the bitch until she finally went away. But she'd come back. That was inevitable.

Something had to be done or I might *never* be free of her. Then I realised my father's words had been a double bluff. The con merchant! He'd been playing me in the knowledge that whatever he said, I'd do the opposite. But I was too smart to fall for his lies.

I stood up, waving and calling out to Maisie as she looked in at me with an awkward grin. I knew then that drawing her in was *precisely* what was needed to resolve the demanding situation that she alone had created. I had to do *whatever* it took to negate the threat she posed. Maisie had brought it on herself. She'd given me no choice. Any guilt was hers and hers alone. So she could hardly blame me for what was to come. I'm sure the panther boy would have agreed with me, were he able to express an opinion. However else could I take back control?

33

I could tell that Maisie was suspicious as soon as she sat in my lounge. She was trying to make out things were normal, feigning interest in my well-being. Asking about my health like she gave a toss. But I knew what she was up to.

'I've been ringing and ringing, Alice, but your phone went straight to messages. I'm your friend as well as your manager. I was desperate to see you. I've been worried sick.'

Like fuck she was! She was poking about, snooping, no more and no less. And now she was looking around my home with those beady eyes and trying to catch me out.

'I'm fine. You've been worrying about nothing.'

'You still don't look well, Alice. What has your doctor said? I don't want you coming back to work until you're fully recovered.'

'My doctor says I'm fine.'

She uncrossed her legs, clearly on edge. No doubt fearing I'd see through her lies. 'You'll need your GP to sign a certificate to that effect before coming back. It's probation department procedure.'

She was seriously pissing me off. I needed a drink. Maybe I should send her on her way after all. I remembered the line my mother had used. It had worked for her. So why not for me? 'I'm, er, I'm getting tired, Maisie. I need to rest. I think it's time you went.'

She stood, still focused on me. Her mouth was opening and closing as if she was trying to say something but unable to express the words. But then, just as I thought I was about to get rid of her, she raised her snooty nose in the air and blurted out the words that made me realise just how much of a threat she truly was.

'I've got to ask, Alice. Is there something wrong with your drains?'

The bitch was onto me. I forced a smile that felt so out of place. My lips moved, but my eyes were cold. I hoped she wouldn't be put on her guard. I calmed my breathing. *Focus, Alice, focus.* 'Ah, yes, I wanted a chat about that. Have you got time for a coffee? I really would appreciate your advice.'

She sat back down. 'Thanks, Alice, that would be lovely. You know how I like it.'

I had her. I *knew* I had her. Now all I had to do was hold my nerve.

'And a biscuit?'

Maisie patted her belly with a convoluted laugh that wasn't convincing anyone. 'I'd better not. Rob's going to be tied up with the murder case for goodness knows how long. My sister's planning a girl's holiday to somewhere in the sun; to Egypt maybe, or the Canaries, I love the north of Tenerife at this time of year. If I don't lose a bit of weight, I'll never fit into my bikini.'

The devious bitch! Why mention the detective again? It was always Rob this or Rob that. She never shut up about him. And *murder*, why call it *murder*? Execution wasn't murder; what the fuck was she talking about?

'How's the investigation going? Has your Rob said anything more?'

Maisie made a face. 'It's not great, to be honest. The police aren't getting anywhere, from what I can gather. Although there is some news, there's another missing sex offender. A young man with an unlawful sexual intercourse conviction. He was eighteen, and the girl was a few weeks short of her sixteenth birthday. The parents insisted on pressing charges, and for some reason the girl gave evidence. There's nothing to suggest the boy's a paedophile. But the police still think he may be another victim of our local killer. They've appealed for information. I don't know if you saw it on the news.'

My world instantly became a darker and more dangerous place. This was yet another thing for me to worry about. What the hell to do? I quickly concluded I should rid myself of the panther boy's remains, and then get rid of Maisie. It was a simple enough system. Destroy the evidence and don't get caught. Focus, don't get rattled, and stick to a plan. I just had to make it happen.

'Let's hope they find him safe and sound.'

'Absolutely! I don't think he's a significant threat to anyone.'

I took a deep breath, releasing it slowly. It was time to move things along. 'Make yourself comfortable, Maisie. I'll go and get that coffee. Open a window if you'd like some fresh air.'

She nodded, looking a little sheepish. 'I think I will, thanks, if you're sure that's okay with you?'

'It's a bit stiff. You'll need to give it a good shove.'

I rushed to my first-floor bathroom, grabbed the plastic tranquilliser bottle from the medicine cabinet on the wall above the sink, and hurried to my cottage kitchen, ensuring my slaughterhouse door was closed tight shut as I went. My chest tightened again as I began preparing the coffee. Would it mask the taste of the drug well enough that the bitch would drink it in sufficient quantity? That concerned me to the point of virtual panic, but a quick swig of vodka helped to settle my nerves as I placed several heaped spoonfuls of a potent Columbian blend into a stainless-steel percolator I hadn't used for many months.

I poured a small amount of the aromatic brown liquid into a white china cup to sample it. I raised it to my lips and sipped. The taste was strong, a complex blend of different flavours, bitter, nutty, and smoky. My hopes were raised as I danced in a circle. Surely my plan would work – something else to be proud of.

I prepared two hot drinks, the china cup for me, black coffee with a little coconut sugar, and then a larger mug for her, with soya milk and a suitably large serving of the sleeping draught, which I stirred in thoroughly. Now for the taste test; yes, not bad, not bad at all, the drug was barely perceptible even to me. If I hadn't known it was there, I really don't think I would have noticed it at all. It was time to go. My plan was inspired. How could it possibly go wrong?

I placed the two coffees on a tarnished, silver-plated tray, and headed back to my lounge, keen to execute my plan in the shortest possible time. The panther boy's body was calling. I wanted to get back to him. His burial could wait for a day or two but no longer than that. There was only so long I could delay removing his remaining tattoos before putting him in the ground.

Maisie had moved her chair a little closer to the half-open window when I returned to the room despite the winter chill. She looked up at me with a misplaced smile as she took her mug from the tray. But she grimaced slightly when she first tasted her coffee. That wasn't good. It wasn't good at all.

I moved my chair nearer to my target. 'Do you like it?'

She took another sip. 'It tastes a little unusual. I think that's the best way of putting it.'

'Ah, yeah, I know what you mean. It's a new Columbian blend. I read about it online. It's all the rage in celebrity circles. I thought someone with your discerning tastes would appreciate it.'

Maisie raised the concoction to her mouth for a third time, swallowing more of it this time, before cradling the mug in both hands, no doubt appreciating the residual warmth as a cold breeze fluttered the curtains. She swallowed again and said she was enjoying it.

Do you find that as hilarious as I do? That's all I had to do, flatter the bitch, feed her ego. She was so easy to influence, so simple to manipulate. Within ten minutes, Maisie had drained her mug and was already yawning. About five minutes later and the stupid bitch's head slumped to one side with a dribble of drool running from her mouth to her chin. Not a good look. I feel sure she'd have hated it. But, no doubt, there'd be worse to come.

I left Maisie flopped in her seat for a few minutes while I finished my coffee in peace with my feet up. There was no point rushing things unnecessarily. Why put pressure on myself?

I closed the window and drew the curtains in the interest of security before trying to lift her dead weight without any hope of succeeding. I took her arm with both hands and pulled her towards me, leaning back, using my weight to move her a few inches at a time until she finally fell to the floor.

As I dragged her sleeping form towards my slaughterhouse, I asked myself why I hadn't killed her already. Why on earth had I created work for myself. Why hadn't I lured her into the killing room and used a knife to get it over quickly? As I laid her alongside the panther boy's decaying corpse, I wondered if my reluctance was due to her gender. I'd never executed a woman. Maybe that was it. Or was it because she wasn't a convicted criminal like my previous guests?

In truth, I struggled to decide if the threats she posed warranted her execution. She'd interfered, yes, she'd stuck her nose in, certainly, but was that enough to justify a death sentence? I eventually decided that she did at least deserve a fair trial before I killed her. I'm too soft for my own good sometimes, that's my problem. I dragged her into a seated position before handcuffing her to the radiator. A good job well done but not yet finished.

I lay down in the arms of my panther boy and whispered sweet nothings.

An hour or two of quiet interlude and I'd be ready to wake her. I'd have to listen to whatever she had to say for herself before deciding her fate.

34

You should have seen the look of shock on Maisie's face after I'd shaken her awake. It was one of the funniest things I'd ever seen. I don't take pleasure in her capture or imprisonment. It was an unavoidable necessity. She gave me no choice. And a small part of me regretted it. I'm not inhuman, after all.

But that look! Her mouth fell open. Her eyes were wide, the whites flashing. And her mascara was smudged across her stupid face. Don't judge me. You weren't there. If you'd seen her, you'd have laughed too.

Maisie looked up at me with her panda eyes, then at the panther boy's decomposing corpse, and then at me again, as if she couldn't quite believe what she was seeing. I'd used almost half a can of air freshener, a lemon blend I was keen to try. But there was still a stink. Maisie wasn't used to such things, as I was. So it's understandable. I do get it, really I do. I could see that her entire body was trembling. And I don't think she thought of me as a friend anymore. How quickly things can change.

I held a glass of cold water to Maisie's mouth, allowing her to drink. It was an act of kindness, a reward for her compliance.

She wasn't tugging at her handcuffs or throwing herself about like some of my previous guests. She'd come to talk. And now she had the opportunity to do exactly that. Maybe that pleased her despite her apparent fear. I like to think it did.

'Would you like something to eat, Maisie? I can spoon something into your mouth if that helps.'

'I'm not hungry, Alice. But I need the toilet. I c-can't hold on much longer. Please l-let me go.'

I smiled and nodded, glad to be able to put her at her ease. 'Just let go where you are. The plastic sheeting will take care of it. Don't worry yourself. You won't soil the floorboards.'

I could see her staring at the panther boy again as the urine pooled around her. Maybe she liked his body art too. That must have been it. She seemed unable to look away.

'Why, Alice, why?'

I found the question so very disappointing. Why didn't she thank me? She didn't seem to appreciate my kindness at all.

'Isn't it obvious?'

She looked me in the eye now while rocking slightly, a fixed expression on her face. 'Did– did you k-kill them all?'

I smiled. She was at least acknowledging my accomplishments. That made me feel proud. I liked her a little more after that.

I pointed towards the panther boy. 'I'm planning to bury him later today. Such a shame, but it's reached that time. I'll put the heating on once he's gone. You'll be more comfortable after that.'

I thought she'd have been delighted. But no, the stuck-up mare still wasn't happy. Some people are never satisfied. I think she's one of those.

'I'm b-begging you, Alice. *Please, please, please* undo my handcuffs. Rob will be l-looking for me. I don't want to d-die. I'm begging you. We're trying for a baby. Please let me go.'

Now the bitch was revealing her true colours. Mentioning her police officer husband yet again. Was she trying to anger me? She'd *never* let it go. I chose to ignore Maisie's ranting as she wailed, so full of self-pity.

I, in contrast, had to consider the bigger picture. It wasn't all about me. I spent the next hour or so disjointing what was left of the panther boy's beautiful body as Maisie watched and wept.

Approximately two hours' hard work and he was buried in my garden, beauty to beauty, food for my roses. I gave him one final peck on the cheek before tossing his decapitated head into the ground.

After moving the convertible, I stumbled back to my cottage, exhausted and aching. I decided on a quick bite to eat and a luxuriously hot bath before looking in on Maisie for one final time that day. I thought it only fair to keep her informed. Her trial would have to wait until morning.

35

I was up early the following morning, having had very little sleep due mainly to my thoughtless guest. Even with the slaughterhouse door shut, I could still hear her wailing. She even started shouting for help at one point in the early hours.

I should probably have gagged her. I had other oranges. But I couldn't be bothered to get up. Dragging myself from bed would have been too much of an effort on such a chilly night. Instead, I relied on night-time drinking and a little sleeping medication from time to time. I suckled on the bottles like a baby on the nipple. Sometimes I have to be kind to myself. I can't always put the needs of others first.

I marched into my slaughterhouse at 9am precisely, a mug of strong coffee in one hand. I hadn't made Maisie a hot drink; she didn't deserve it for obvious reasons. But I knew I'd need the stimulation the caffeine offered as her trial began.

When Maisie started pleading, I had to slap her hard. I had to shut the silly bitch up somehow. There was only so much I could put up with, and it seemed the easiest way. I'd put the heating on, and the room was warmer. But she didn't appreciate the comfort it offered one little bit. She's a crazy woman, so very ungrateful. Enough was most definitely enough.

'Why did you come here, Maisie? Think *very* carefully before you answer. I require the truth and nothing but the truth. Think of this as a court of your peers.'

'*Please* let me go. I haven't done a-anything to d-deserve this. We're friends, aren't we? *Please* let m-me go.'

She had such a whiney voice, so very irritating. I threw my hot coffee in her face.

'Answer the fucking question!'

Maisie shook her head like a wet dog, blinking the coffee away. 'You collapsed in f-front of me. You've been ill. I wanted t-to make sure you're o-okay.'

I yelled my response. 'Am I supposed to believe that crap? And stop your fucking stuttering!'

'I brought you a c-card and s-some flowers. They're in the boot of my c-car. Why n-not take a look? You'll see it's t-true.'

I leapt forward, drawing my arm back and slapping her for the second time, this time to the side of her head, stinging her ear. 'I'll ask the questions. You're not the boss now.'

She lowered her voice in pitch and tone. 'All right, Alice, you're in charge, anything y-you say. I had to visit b-because of my duty of c-care as your manager. It's written in the procedures. It's something I *had* to do. I wouldn't have bothered y-you otherwise.'

I bent at the waist, placing my face only inches from hers. 'You were *snooping*, Maisie. Sticking your beaky nose in where it doesn't belong.'

And then she lost control of her mouth as I stood above her. 'Did you kill them all?'

I beamed with pride. 'The ones you know about and others. The past calls out to us. I'm a rat catcher, a killer of vermin. It all began with my father and continued from there.'

Maisie didn't speak for a while after that. She just sat there, whimpering. And when she did finally speak, she spoke slowly, as if carefully selecting each word, almost in slow motion. As if that would somehow make it more acceptable to me. She was so full of crap, one lie after another. 'I know why you did it, Alice. They were b-bad men who did terrible things. The police would get that too, and the court. I could be a character witness. I can help y-you if you let me.'

I had to laugh. She'd got it so horribly wrong. 'But I don't want your help, Maisie. I don't want to stop. There's any number of monsters I still need to target and execute. You should know that better than most. The system you're part of doesn't work. And now you're here interfering with my quest, getting in the way at the worst possible time. It's almost as if you're on the side of the beasts, not mine. Is that true, Maisie? Is that what's happening here? I think it is. You're as guilty as sin.'

'No, no, I get it; honestly, I d-do. I could help you identify suitable victims. Just undo m-my handcuffs. I won't s-say a word to anybody. We could k-kill the criminals together; you and me against the world. Us girls have got to stick together. Do you remember?'

I felt so horribly let down, so utterly disappointed in Maisie. It was so self-evident that she'd say *anything* to save herself. The woman had no integrity, no strong moral principles. We were so very different. I knew then that any further questions were pointless. I picked up my utility knife intending to cut her throat. But as I knelt at her side, I found I couldn't do it.

Maybe it would be different if I was drunk. Perhaps then I could kill her. Or perhaps I should let her live for a day or two longer. I decided to leave her sitting there in her filth until the next day and then try again.

But I couldn't stand to hear her incessant wailing for another minute. I took my hammer and hit her once. Crack! At the front of her skull three inches above her eyebrows. Maisie slumped forward as far as her secured arms would allow. She was unconscious but still breathing – one more thing to be proud of. I'd judged the blow just right.

36

The next day began surprisingly well. The sun was shining when I opened my bedroom curtains, the birds were singing, and I'd slept for almost eight hours, only waking once. That was unusual for me. For once I'd experienced no nightmares or flashbacks, and my poisonous father hadn't made even a single appearance. There'd been no hand on my door handle, and no voice in my ear. That was something to celebrate. I even performed a few physical exercises before heading to the bathroom at a little after 7am.

I brushed my teeth, emptied my bladder, and showered in a festive mood, singing a favourite song as I lathered my body with scented soap, taking sensual pleasure in hot water warming my skin. I was keenly anticipating looking in on Maisie before breakfast. It was going to be a momentous day for both of us.

I'd decided to keep her alive for a day or two longer while I pumped her for information, and I was happily anticipating telling her the good news. I'd also decided to hold a garden ceremony of remembrance for my panther boy. I have to admit I was missing him more than I'd anticipated. We'd formed a rare bond born of adversity. I think in very different circumstances we may have become even closer than we did. I'm not saying we'd have married, had children, and lived happily ever after or anything as ridiculously romantic as that. But we may well have enjoyed a meaningful relationship based on our shared experience.

What a shame it wasn't meant to be. I'll always regret that to some extent. But at least I'll have that incredible framed tattoo on my lounge wall. What a marvellous reminder of a boy I feel privileged to have known, however short the time we spent together. He was far from perfect, but he recognised his flaws and was willing to learn from them. With my help, he could have been redeemable. He may even have joined me in my quest.

We could have become a double act, executing the evil wrongdoers together. Wow! I never thought I'd find myself saying that of any man, however young and inexperienced. But, of course, I couldn't take that risk. What if he'd betrayed me? It could have happened. People let you down. I know that better than most. I can only rely on myself, just me and my reflection.

Killing the panther boy softly was the only possible course of action left open to me. My work has to continue. Allowing him to get in the way of that could have ended in disaster. I couldn't let that happen. He had to die one way or another.

Maisie was still slumped, handcuffed to the radiator where I'd left her when I checked in on her on my way to the kitchen. When I first saw her, I thought she might have died during the night. She had that sallow yellow look about her that corpses often have. But, no, her chest was moving up and down ever so slightly when I studied her closely. I even held a hand-mirror to her face to confirm my assessment. And, yes, her breath clouded the glass.

I closed my slaughterhouse door with a skip in my step and

entered my cottage kitchen with an appetite that needed to be satisfied.

I cooked fried eggs, button mushrooms and ripe tomatoes, heaping the delicious, greasy fare onto my plate, looking forward to eating it for a change. I have no idea where that new culinary enthusiasm came from. A strong coffee laced with a little blended whisky, and I was feeling even more positive as I stepped out into my rose garden, enjoying the morning sun on my face. There was a slight but discernible warmth in the air for the first time that year.

Maybe my good mood was because spring was on its merry way. New life was appearing. The daffodil's green shoots were already poking through the dark soil with their closed yellow heads, and I felt sure that my panther boy now appreciated his new underground home. How could he not? The scene was so stunning – the Welsh countryside at its glorious best.

I was about to head back into my cottage to wake Maisie from her enforced slumber when the morning went from good to better. I heard the delivery van before seeing it. There it was coming down my track, approaching my home. I met the driver in my yard and smiled with genuine pleasure as he handed me my carefully packaged picture frame through the open window of his vehicle.

'There you go, love, that one's for you. It's nice to see the sun shining.'

I could hardly contain my excitement as I held the parcel in both hands. I looked up at the sky with my eyes narrowed. The sun was low but still bright, coming over the trees. He was right; it was nice to see it shining in a pale-blue sky almost free of clouds.

'Yes, it is, it's a wonderful day.'

'I'll see you again, love.'

I felt myself tense. What the hell did he mean by that? I

turned away, rushing towards my front door as the potential threat prepared to drive away. I concluded I was well rid of him. If he came again, I wouldn't talk to him at all. Maybe a drink to settle my nerves. Yes, why not? I couldn't let the bastard lower my mood.

It took me almost half an hour to frame that awesome panther tattoo to my eventual satisfaction. I had to trim the skin ever so slightly at the edges. But it was very well worth the effort. It looked genuinely fantastic by the time I'd finished. I retrieved my hammer from the slaughterhouse floor, fetched a suitable masonry nail from my garden shed, and hung my new picture on the lounge wall next to my degree certificate. I stood back to admire it with pride for a full minute. It was such an excellent way to remember such a lovely boy. I'm sure he'd appreciate it, were he alive to see it, almost as much as I did. I wish I could show it to you. My words don't do it justice. He was even more beautiful in death than he had been in life. My new panther tattoo looked even better in the frame than it had on him.

A bucket of cold water and Maisie was awake a few minutes later. Not sharp in the sense I was. She was still groggy and somewhat confused when I tried to speak to her.

I considered releasing her handcuffs, to take her to my lounge, to show her my picture. But in the end, I decided it made more sense to bring it to her. I really thought she'd be interested, that she'd appreciate my generous gesture, that she'd be glad that I'd involved her at all. It's not like I had to. It was another moment of kindness on my part. I was reaching out to her out of the goodness of my heart.

But that's when my day took a darker turn. Maisie lost control of her bowel as I held the picture up in front of her. And then she vomited. Right there and then all over herself. Can you believe that? After everything I'd done for her. The woman is a total and utter disgrace.

Another two buckets of cold water and she was reasonably clean again. And she uttered a word or two. I couldn't make sense of what she was saying, but she was trying to speak. I was glad of that, communication matters. I told her I'd probably kill her sometime that afternoon.

I ate an early lunch after rehanging my picture, with less gusto than I had breakfast. My mood was lower by then, no doubt due to Maisie's unfortunate lack of enthusiasm and that unpleasant delivery driver who'd upset me in the way men so often do. But I concluded that those unpleasantries would give me the motivation to get the job done. I like to be flexible, as I've said before. Maisie had to die. I was no longer enjoying her company. And she was very obviously guilty. There was no doubt on that score. So, why delay her execution?

I threw my dirty plate and cutlery into the sink before heading towards my slaughterhouse, striding out with a new determination to end Maisie's life and the threat she posed. But as I entered the hall, I dropped quickly to my knees as the silhouette of a woman I felt sure I recognised approached my front door. I hurried over the tiles on all fours as she began knocking. And then I crawled into my lounge to hide behind the sofa, hoping she'd go away.

But Detective Inspector Laura Kesey wasn't a woman who gave up easily. She pushed open my half-closed lounge window, placing her head through the resulting gap.

'Hello, Alice, it's DI Kesey, Laura Kesey, it's the police. I'd like a word with you.'

My father made an inevitable appearance at that precise moment, no surprises there. He could not wait to mock me. No doubt he'd been anticipating this moment since the day of my first execution. The bastard must have been creaming his pants.

It's the police, Alice, and they've come for you. You'll be taken away. Oh, dear, how very sad, it's all downhill from here.

I hissed my reply for fear that the piggy officer may overhear. 'Get back to hell!'

I chose to ignore my father's resulting sneer. I've got used to such things. But what to do? What the hell to do? I had to think quickly. The slaughterhouse door was closed. Maisie was silent. Maybe I should let the detective in. Perhaps I could bluff it out.

As she tapped the window insistently, I knew I had to face her. It could work out okay, couldn't it? The little Midlands piggy was alone. Surely that was a good sign, wasn't it? She could be visiting for any number of reasons. Officers hunted in packs where major investigations were concerned. I hurriedly crawled back toward the hall just after Kesey turned away.

A few seconds later, I opened the front door, calling out to her. 'Hi, Laura, I thought it was you. I was upstairs in the bathroom. Sorry to keep you waiting. What can I do for you?'

The professional snooper stared back at me with her small, round eyes. 'Can I come in for a quick chat?'

How to play it? 'I was about to go out.'

She took a step towards me. 'I won't keep you long. But we *do* need to talk. We can do it here or inside. It's up to you.'

That concerned me. If I'd been holding a knife, I'd probably have stabbed her right there and then. To get it over with. 'I'll put the kettle on if you fancy a coffee.'

'Not for me, thanks. I haven't long had one.'

Shit! For fuck's sake! That ruled out the sleeping draught. My head pounded as I led her into my lounge. Fortunately, the window was open. There was still a slight odour, but it wasn't overpowering.

'Take a seat, Laura. Do you need another statement? I'm sure I've already told you all I know. But I'm always ready to help if I can.'

'I'm looking for Maisie. She didn't arrive home yesterday

evening. The last time her partner spoke to her, she said she was coming here.'

My mind was racing, the cogs turning faster and faster. *What the hell to say? What the fuck to do? Shut up, Father. Shut the fuck up! I need to concentrate.* 'That's strange; what sort of time would she have been here?'

'It would have been sometime yesterday morning. I can't be more specific than that.'

'Ah, okay, that makes sense. I went out for a long drive straight after breakfast. I ended up on the Beacons. I didn't get back until gone three.'

And I really thought that was it as the piggy detective rose to her feet preparing to leave. It seemed I'd deceived her as I had that young female uniformed officer so very long ago. But then Kesey suddenly looked up at the newly framed picture hanging on my wall above the fireplace, as if she was registering it for the very first time. Her face turned ashen as she stopped and stared, and I knew in that instant that my life had changed forever. She knew what it was. She knew where it was from. It was fight or flight, but I had nowhere to run. I edged towards the door to the hall, fully intending to grasp a suitable weapon from my slaughterhouse floor. But then she spoke in that Midlands drone of hers, and for some reason, I turned to listen. I still can't understand why, but I did.

She pointed at my black panther with a fixed expression that said a thousand words. 'What's that?'

I moved a little closer to the door, but I didn't reply. There was nothing I could have said to change anything for the better. I knew from her face that she wouldn't understand. And then I ran, suddenly, like a sprinter off the blocks, shoving my slaughterhouse door open with my leading shoulder as she came after me. I reached down, picking up my hammer, the only weapon within my easy reach as the piggy detective entered the room. Kesey looked at me, then at Maisie handcuffed to that black Victorian radiator, and then at me again, her eyes wide as if she couldn't quite believe what she was seeing. She fumbled for her phone, clutching it in her right hand while holding her left out as if stopping traffic.

'Stay where you are, Alice. Drop the hammer. It's over. You're in enough trouble without making things even worse for yourself.'

I lunged at the piggy detective as she went to dial, covering the ground between us in two rapid strides, knocking her smartphone to the floor before stamping down on it, cracking the glass. She let out a scream as she jumped in the air, kicking out at me karate style, hitting my hammer arm with a powerful blow just above my elbow. The strike sent me staggering sideways, but I somehow held onto my weapon.

What I've since learnt but didn't know then is that Kesey has a black belt. She's represented the UK in international competition. It wouldn't have made a difference to my actions. I had no choice but to fight. But I've no doubt it tilted the odds in her favour. If I'd had a gun, I'd have blown her fucking head off.

My arm ached as I raised the hammer high above my head, attempting to strike her. But she moved with speed and grace, throwing out three fast jabs and landing another kick, this time to my left thigh, a few inches above my knee. I knew then that I wasn't fighting any ordinary opponent. None of my previous visitors had a similar level of combat skills, not even Simpson, who was the best of the rest.

As Kesey picked up her phone, I could see she was out of breath. That gave me hope. But as she moved away from me, I wasn't nearly quick enough to stop her dialling. I did manage to land a glancing blow to her shoulder, making her wince, but the bitch had already summoned help. I hated her for that. I wanted to tear her apart. To make her suffer as she'd never suffered before. We should have been on the same side. She was tormenting the wrong person. Why didn't she realise that? It seems so obvious to me.

Father began laughing somewhere behind me as I failed to land a wild blow to her skull. She then swept me; I think that's the technical term, dropping to the floor and kicking hard in one rapid movement, taking out both my legs from under me. I was in mid-air for a fraction of a second before landing heavily on my coccyx. A stab of pain exploded up my spine as the bitch spun me onto my front before forcing my hammer arm high up my back until I dropped my weapon.

We were both panting hard as she sat astride me, still pinning my arm with the one hand while gripping the hair at the back of my head with the other. She jerked my head back and held it there as she told me I was being arrested on suspicion of murder. I struggled but without any success. She was more skilled than me and very probably stronger. I hadn't felt so helpless since being a child. It was as if I was being abused all over again.

I thought that Kesey might have broken my arm at one point. I let out a yell of pain and a string of expletives. I tried to reason with her, but she didn't want to hear it. She said no more. She just held me there until we finally heard sirens about fifteen minutes later.

I listened to the crashing of the front door being forced open as Kesey called out to her arriving colleagues. Within seconds I was being dragged towards a police car by two burly male uniformed officers who threw me into the back seat with such force that I bounced off the opposite door. An ambulance sped down my track and into the yard as one of the two officers prepared to drive off to the police station. As I looked back, I saw Kesey meeting the paramedics at my broken door, hurriedly ushering them into the cottage as if Maisie's life was more important than mine. Now I knew my quest was over. I'd have to face a confused and misunderstanding world who saw my actions as crimes for some bizarre reason I still can't understand.

I swore loudly and crudely as I thought of my rose garden, my thwarted plans, and then of my panther tattoo. I'd lost so very much in such a short time. And there were so many more monster men out there in the world whom I should have trapped and destroyed. I began to cry, experiencing a crushing sense of failure.

I told you so, Alice, I told you.

'Shut up, Father, shut the fuck up!'

It seemed he might have been right all along.

37

The world had gone mad. I was forced to see a doctor in my police cell the morning after my arrest. I needed assessing, apparently. How crazy is that? A man claiming to be the principal police surgeon for the county asked me all sorts of ridiculous questions. He even asked if I heard voices just because I spoke to my father.

And I really think the fool doubted my competence. Because I clearly heard him tell Kesey that I'd need an appropriate adult to sit in on my interview as well as a solicitor. That annoyed me more than I can say. I yelled a stream of angry abuse at the two of them as they stood talking outside my cell door. But it seemed neither Kesey nor the doctor wanted to listen to a single word I said. It was as if I was a non-person, worthless, of no importance at all. They just walked off without further acknowledging my complaints – bad manners at their very worst. The legal system is a total disgrace. No wonder there's so many miscarriages of justice. I now don't trust the police at all.

I was formally interviewed about an hour later. There was me, DI Kesey, that same DS Lewis who'd sat alongside her in the press conference, a middle-aged female social worker who claimed to be there to support, advise and assist me, a young duty solicitor in a crumpled grey business suit that looked older than he did, and finally my father. Everyone was seated in the small, claustrophobic room, except for my father, who chose to hover in the background, coming in and out of focus as he chose. And the strange thing was that no one else seemed to see or hear him but me. I couldn't make sense of that. Although, it may have been a professional conspiracy to unnerve me. To make me doubt my sanity.

Kesey and Lewis sat across the interview room table from me and my allocated supporters, team Alice against team police. Both the piggy officers stared into my face for what felt like an age before Kesey finally spoke, taking the lead as befitted her rank. I was just glad the silence had ended. Silence makes me overthink. And that can be a problem.

'Switch on the tape, please, Ray. It's time we made a start.'

'Will do, ma'am.'

Why so formal? I think they were playing games. I grinned as Kesey focused on me again. It was an interesting process. And Father seemed just as fascinated as I was. In different circumstances, he may have faced such an interview. We were both wondering what on earth the piggy detective was going to say next.

'I want to remind you that you're still subject to caution, Miss Granger. You do not have to say anything, but it may harm your defence if you do not mention when questioned something that you later rely on in court. Anything you do say may be given in evidence. Do you understand?'

I glanced toward my idiot lawyer, holding his gaze for a second or two before suddenly looking away. 'This whole process is a complete farce. Why the hell would I go to court? You should be applauding me. I've done nothing but good.'

Kesey rested her elbows on the tabletop, leaning towards me.

I could feel her breath on my face. 'You've been arrested on suspicion of murder, Alice. Scenes of crimes officers are already examining every inch of your cottage and garden. Human remains have already been found. This is your opportunity to tell us your side of the story in your own words. I need you to confirm that you understand the caution before we continue the interview.'

I nodded once, but it seems that wasn't nearly good enough for the stuck-up bitch.

'Confirm it for the tape, please, Alice. I need to hear you say it.'

Her implied lack of respect irritated the crap out of me. I could quite easily have slapped her and slapped her hard. It would have felt so delicious. 'I work for the probation department. Of course I understand. I don't know why you even feel the need to ask. Show some respect. I wish I'd caved your head in when I had the chance.'

My inept solicitor started chattering in my ear at that point as if I didn't have enough to deal with. I told him to shut his stupid mouth. There was no point in the idiot being there at all. The appropriate adult stuck her nose in too. She said I should listen to my lawyer. That he was there to help me. I told her to fuck off. I yelled it in her face. What did she know? They were two more big-mouthed twats dragging me down. As if my father wasn't enough of a burden to deal with. I jumped up, shaking a fist at that black-clad purveyor of gloom as he hovered behind the two officers making faces.

Kesey took my arm, sitting me back down. 'Did you hear what I said, Alice? Human remains have been found both inside and outside your property. What have you got to say about that?'

I sighed dramatically, starting to get bored. And I needed a drink. I *so* needed a drink. But that was never going to happen. I pictured Kesey's decapitated head impaled on a spike and felt a little better. 'What's the big deal? Can't we get this shit over with?'

'We have evidence to suggest that you've killed several victims at your home address. What have you got to say in response?'

That both amused and angered me. She already knew *exactly* what I'd done. Why waste my time? And calling them victims, outrageous! My idiot lawyer tried to interrupt again, but I put him in his place. Maybe if I'd had the chance, I'd have killed him too. 'There are five bodies in my garden – four monsters and a young man who I became rather fond of before the end. You'll find them all under the rose bushes if you haven't already. And then, of course, there's the head the farmer found. The rest of the monster's body is somewhere in the river along with another.

'And before you ask, I'm proud of what I've done. I executed nonces, monsters in human form. I made the world a better place. The young man with the straw-yellow hair, panther tattoo and sky-blue eyes is my only slight regret. I would have let him live was I able to. That was such a shame. Although I made certain he didn't suffer, unlike the others, who went through hell on earth. I hope they're suffering still, burning for eternity. If there is a netherworld somewhere in infinity, it's full of monster men like them, destroyers of innocence. I'm on the side of the angels.'

The two piggy detectives glanced at each other before DS Lewis spoke for the first time. I'd been beginning to wonder if he spoke at all. 'We'll need to go through the details of each killing in turn. And then the probation officer's imprisonment and assault. We'll need to talk about that too.'

I relaxed back in my chair. 'How is Maisie?'

It seemed no one wanted to answer.

'Let's start at the beginning. When did you murder your first victim?'

I slammed an open palm down on the table, raising my voice almost to a shout. 'Let's get two things straight before we continue this shit. One, they weren't victims. They were beasts in need of slaying. And two, I didn't murder anyone. They were *executions*, justified *executions* following a trial and sentence. I need you to understand that. I'm not saying another word until you do.'

Lewis took a deep breath, sucking in the air. 'Okay, let's start again. When did you carry out your first execution?'

I then spent almost two hours going through each of the killings in turn. The idiot solicitor, the appropriate adult, Kesey, and, of course, my demented father all interrupted from time to time, much to my frustration and annoyance. But the majority of my conversation was with Lewis. And I came to enjoy the sharing. I got the distinct impression that the ageing detective sergeant was a good man, not one of life's many monsters. I think he would have applauded me if he could have. I talked him through the entire process, starting with my father and ending with my panther boy.

I told my story with pride and passion, as I do to you now. The others sat there in stunned silence as I told Lewis how it all started. Why and how I killed my father and everything that came after. I explained my planning process, how I identified my targets, and how I lured them to my cottage. When I talked of the monsters' trials and punishments, I saw Kesey shudder. Although, I got the distinct impression that Lewis retained his composure throughout our entire discussion. I think he got it, my reasoning, why I acted as I did. He couldn't say that, not in that setting. But in different circumstances, I think Lewis would have liked to eliminate monsters as I had if he embraced his true self.

Lewis thanked me when I ended my dynamic presentation with a flourish. He showed me the respect I deserved. And then I was charged, with the executions and with Maisie's imprisonment and punishment too. They called it GBH with intent.

They even plan to prosecute me for alleged offences against Kesey. I guess that was inevitable. It's how the system works. Kesey said I'd never see the light of day again after my new sergeant friend switched off the recording equipment. She claimed I'd face a whole life sentence as a serial killer, that they'd throw away the key. It felt almost personal. As if she was heavily invested in the outcome of my case. But only death and taxes are a certainty in this life. I shrugged as I was marched back to my cell. Kesey was in for a surprise or two before my story ended. The future was far from sure.

38

My Crown Court trial was a case of mad or bad. Or, at least, that's what my supposedly eminent barrister claimed in a pompous, plum-in-the-mouth voice that seemed to define him.

I was vehemently against the idea of pleading not guilty on the grounds of diminished responsibility at first. I wanted to stand up in court and take credit for my actions loud and proud.

But then I thought, *Hang on, maybe it wasn't such a bad idea after all.* Escaping from prison seemed highly unlikely. But a hospital, even a secure hospital, now that offered possibilities. Doctors could be easy to deceive. I could use that to my advantage. I decided to play the game.

It wasn't a case of whether I'd carried out the executions. I freely admitted that I had. I said it in the witness box on oath for all to hear. I told everyone what I'd done and why I did it too. There was a wealth of evidence against me. Both my full confession and the forensic evidence was undeniable. The prosecution barrister even showed the court my framed panther tattoo. It was so good to see it again. The colours were still bright, the frame as striking as I remembered it. It brought me close to tears.

As lengthy and complex as the process was, everything came down to one thing. A jury of my peers, five men and seven women, none of whom knew the truth, had the responsibility of deciding if I could be considered culpable in law. They held my future in their hands. The court process is like a high-stake game of chess, adversarial. I'd been assessed by two supposedly expert witnesses, both consultant psychiatrists, one for the defence and one for the prosecution. Their opinions were dramatically diverse. My defence counsel argued that I was in fact, mentally ill, as stated by our expert. He worked hard to convince the jury of that reality. The prosecution's expert, in contrast, thought I was exaggerating my symptoms. The prosecution counsel said as much, arguing that I was guilty of multiple murders, that I knew exactly what I was doing and should pay the price for my crimes.

I, of course, knew that I was neither mad nor bad. But there seemed little purpose in me trying to argue that point in the witness box. No one wanted to hear it. The strange thing was that I'd been nothing but honest during the pre-trial interviews with both psychiatric doctors. I know I'm sane. You know that I'm sane. But both experts got it horribly wrong. That introduced doubts in the juror's minds. I knew that the best I could hope for was a stay in a secure hospital. So that's what I set out to achieve.

I put on a show in the witness box, twitching, whistling, and giving ludicrous answers to questions asked by both barristers. I talked to my father often, not because I was mad but because he was there. I noticed that those interactions had an impact on the jury. They couldn't hear him. They couldn't see him as I could. And so I exaggerated those conversations, still talking to Father even after he'd left the courtroom. I called out to him, I had non-existent arguments, and I threw punches at the air. When I shouted heartfelt abuse at the judge, he ordered that I was returned to the cells when I refused to shut up. And that was a good thing. I played the game and won.

The jury found me not guilty of murder by a majority verdict after over five hours of deliberation. I'd be off to a secure hospital: no prison for me. I smiled as I was escorted from the building. If I could con the court, I could trick the hospital staff too. It would be all about planning. All about attention to detail. I couldn't be sure I'd succeed in escaping. But deception was something I was good at. I was certain I was going to try.

39

You may have realised by now that I have written the last few chapters of my tale in my new hospital home rather than my much-loved cottage. I have my own room in a secure wing of a faded Victorian building in need of updating. I won't name the institution, but it's well known, notorious even. I'm sure you can work it out if you feel the need. It's in the news often enough.

I miss my cottage terribly and can never return. It saddens me to write those words even now. I only have my memories. The place was put up for sale after the bodies were removed for forensic reasons and later burial. There's still not much interest from buyers. Some of the locals even want the cottage destroyed, wiped off the face of the earth as if it never existed. There's even an online petition signed by a surprising number of people. I've no idea why. What a strange world we live in, it seemed so very idyllic to me.

I was in the hospital for almost five months before finally starting to write again. It took a good deal of persuasion on my part. But a hospital psychologist I saw twice a week for what she liked to call 'therapy sessions' finally agreed. She even helped facilitate the process with my allocated consultant, reasoning that my writing would help me better understand and take moral responsibility for the events that led me to the hospital's door.

I had to use a pen and paper, no more dictation, regrettably. But I was glad I could write at all. I no longer had access to my computer. That was long gone. But thankfully I'd squirrelled my story away deep in the Cloud where I was sure only I could access it. And so my musings weren't lost forever.

Dr Sandler, that's the psychologist's name, Dr Tracy Sandler, even allowed me to print off my manuscript in the secure hospital's library, where I was given access to a computer. That sheaf of papers became my most treasured possession. I guarded it with my life. It was all I had left of my quest. I even let Dr Sandler read it a chapter at a time, although, of course, it wasn't finished then.

Each week I saw Dr Sandler in her comfortable office. And each week we discussed what she'd read. The psychologist claimed she understood why my life had taken the direction it had. Why I'd done the things I did. Why I became the woman I became. And she thought she could help me come to terms with my past. To overcome my traumas to the benefit of my mental health. But for all her paper qualifications, proudly displayed on her office walls, she got everything so very irrevocably wrong. You see, she never understood that my actions were worthy. She failed to comprehend the fact that I'd do it all over again if I got even the slightest chance. And so I used that against her.

I played her misguided games; I thanked her for her input. I said that I was grateful and that I was beginning to understand the gravity of my behaviour for the first time. In short, I worked at gaining her trust, much as I had with Maisie before I smashed her head with my hammer. I shared information with the good doctor because it served my purpose to do so. And it wasn't difficult to pull the wool over her oh-so naive eyes.

I did as Simpson had with his parole board, and as others have too. I told Dr Sandler that she was helping me. That I was no longer hearing my father's voice. And that I now regretted my crimes. I actually called my actions *crimes*. Can you believe that? That almost stuck in my throat. But I had to say it. I had to keep up the act. It was my only way out of there. And that was my sole focus. So, I chose my words with care. I told Dr Sandler exactly what I needed her to hear. And I think she came to like me in the end. I believe she looked forward to our time together. She swallowed all my lies.

I've no doubt she saw me as one of her success stories. A woman who recognised the wrongs of her past and wanted to work towards a different future. She even said that one day I might be released. It wouldn't be soon. I was facing years in that place, not months or even weeks as I'd hoped. The good doctor thought I'd be pleased with that offer of hope. She obviously saw it as a positive. As if she'd told me the world's most excellent news. But I hated her for that. Being freed one day, in God knows how long, wasn't nearly good enough for me. I had to think of the children. Of the monster men still free to spawn their horrors while I sat incarcerated for no good reason at all. And so I looked for opportunities – chances to escape. I came up with one plan and then another. But the hospital's security systems were surprisingly effective. I started to lose hope. And then just when I'd almost given up, it happened, fate smiled on me, the universe conspired in my favour. Maybe there is a God after all.

I was sitting in my hospital room one evening, reading the story of the escape from Alcatraz, when I heard a knock on my door, followed by the sound of a key turning in the lock. I looked up to see Dr Sandler standing there in the company of a male nurse wearing a crumpled uniform, who was stood a few feet behind her.

'Is it okay if I come in to talk, Alice? I'm afraid I have some bad news.'

I invited her in and told her to sit while the nurse stayed standing in the open doorway.

Dr Sandler stretched out an arm, gripping my hand. 'I'm so very sorry to tell you this, Alice. But we've just been notified that your mother has passed away.'

It wasn't a great surprise, I'd been expecting it, but the news still stung. 'What happened?'

She lowered her head momentarily, but then raised it again, re-establishing eye contact. I think that must have been part of her training.

'It was the cancer. Your mother was on a great deal of pain medication. In the end, her heart couldn't take it. She died in her sleep about an hour ago.'

And as my psychologist sat there opposite me in that small secure room, seemingly close to tears, I saw an opportunity. Mother's death would mean a funeral, a service back in Wales, very probably at the same crematorium with which I'd become familiar as a teenager. I began to cry, more for effect than anything else. 'Will there be a post-mortem?'

She shook her head. 'No, that won't be necessary, not in the circumstances. Your mother's death was expected. She died in hospital. A doctor will have signed her death certificate. I'm so very sorry to give you such bad news. Please accept my sympathies for your loss.'

I rubbed my eyes with the back of one hand. 'Mother was a wonderful woman. Thank you for your kind words.'

'Yes, yes, I enjoyed reading about her in your diary. It's good that the two of you resolved your differences at your last meeting.'

'I forgave her.'

The psychologist patted my arm, a tear in her eye. 'Yes, you did, Alice, and that's to your absolute credit. I feel sure that your mum truly appreciated your generosity of spirit. And I'm certain she found peace before she passed. You will, too, once you've had the time to grieve.'

Dr Sandler was so full of shit.

'Will there be a funeral?'

She raised her eyebrows, eyelids open, brow furrowed. She has one of those faces which only ever mirror what she's thinking. I'm so very glad I'm not like that. I don't think she had the slightest clue what I was planning. I needed to keep it that way.

'Um, yes, absolutely, once the death is registered.'

'I should be arranging the funeral. I know what she'd want. Who should be there. It's something we talked about at that last visit.'

'I'm afraid that's not going to be possible, Alice. Surely there must be someone else who can make the necessary arrangements.'

I was silent for a few seconds, staring into the unseen distance as if I could see through walls. 'There's my maternal grandmother, I guess; my sister's far too young. Oh, God, she's going to be heartbroken. I really would like to speak to them both. I should be there for them. It would mean a lot to them and to me too. That's what my mother would have wanted.'

Call herself a psychologist. Ha! She was so gullible, so naive. I was playing her to perfection, steering the conversation at will. 'I'll see if I can arrange a phone call. I can't see it being a problem, what with the circumstances. There are procedures to consider. I'll need to discuss it with your consultant. But I'm sure I can set something up for tomorrow morning.'

'I doubt Dr Barnes will object. He said I'm making excellent progress.'

She nodded with a smile. 'I'm sure you're right. You are doing well, Alice. Your mother would have been proud.'

I tensed as she stood to leave.

'There is one more thing I'd like to discuss, Dr Sandler.'

She glanced at her watch. 'What is it?'

'I'd *really* like to go to the funeral. She was my mother, after all. You only get one. The idea of not being there for her fills me with horror. I don't think it's something I could cope with.'

She looked far from persuaded, but she didn't say no. 'I'll have to talk to Dr Barnes. Let's see what he says.'

I felt like cheering but hid it well. She was a stupid bitch. She didn't have a fucking clue. And that suited me just fine.

'Thank you so very much, doctor. I truly appreciate your help. You've been a wonderful therapist to me. Had I met you as a child, my life could have been very different.'

She smiled. 'I'll arrange that phone call for the morning.'

'Thank you.'

'You're welcome.'

I pressed my face into my pillow, giggling as Dr Sandler closed my door and walked away, the male nurse scuttling along behind her like an obedient puppy snapping at her heels. Soon I'd have my chance. Yes, I'd have my opportunity. Now all I had to do was make it count.

40

I'd had my promised phone conversation with my maternal grandmother by the time I joined Dr Sandler for my next scheduled therapy session two days later. The call was short but sweet and poorly supervised too, by another male nurse who stood on the other side of a glass panelled door, absent-mindedly picking his nose, as I spoke quietly out of his hearing. I said what I needed to say. I told her what I needed her to do. And my grandmother was receptive.

'I didn't believe a word they said about you, Alice. It's a miscarriage of justice. I'll do all I can to help you. It's what your mother would have wanted. It's so good to hear your voice.'

My grandmother was in complete denial, which made life easier for both of us. She'd arrange the funeral at that same crematorium, and she'd look after my little sister. I was genuinely pleased about that. But best of all she'd follow my instructions to the letter. She'd said as much. All was well if I could just get to the funeral. That was the key to my plan. Everything else would almost look after itself.

I hadn't yet repeated my wish to attend the service, not to Dr Sandler, not to anyone who mattered. I needed to time the request exactly right to maximise my chances of success. And I was nervous. I'm not frightened to admit that. Opportunities like that don't come along very often. It truly mattered.

As we sat there in her office discussing my writing, I soon realised that the session might provide me with an ideal chance to achieve my ultimate goal. Dr Sandler was in an unusually positive mood. She was particularly pleased that I'd expressed regret for what she saw as my crimes. And she was even more gratified that I'd said I now found some chapters of my memoirs even more distressing to read than she did. I'd been selective of what I'd shown her, of course, I chose what suited my purpose. And I planned what to say too. Preparation is everything.

'The chapter describing poor Simpson's death was deeply upsetting for me to read, doctor. I can't believe I did those awful things to that poor man. He was a human being with rights. I can see that now. If I ever get out of here, I'll strive to be a better person for the rest of my life; and that's largely because of you.'

She smiled and preened, congratulating me on my honesty and insight. It seemed that my statement was an excellent foundation for positive change. Or, at least, that's what she thought in her confused world of self-serving delusion. How hilarious is that? I, in contrast, had very different ideas. Not that I was ever going to tell her that.

Instead, I asked her if there was any news of Maisie. It was a question I often asked. Not because I cared about the answer, but because it created an image of myself that I wanted to portray. It was a part of my disguise, my mask. To my surprise, for the first time, the good doctor had a meaningful reply to offer.

She'd been in touch with the probation service. Maisie, it seemed was back in work after a lengthy period of sick leave. I couldn't have given a toss, that's real honesty. Maisie let me down, after all. But I said that I was relieved and gratified by the good news. I even offered to write a letter of apology to my old boss expressing my deep regret for what I'd done to her. Dr Sandler thought it a good idea but said that she'd have to ask Maisie if it was acceptable to her.

'I understand completely, doctor. It has to be about Maisie's needs, not mine. I only hope she can put what happened behind her and get on with her life. It would mean the world to me if she could.'

'Do you ever hear your father's voice anymore?'

'No, never, it's amazing how much progress I've made.'

'That's good to hear, Alice. And what about your desire for alcohol?'

'The cravings have almost gone.'

She gave a little clap of delight, like a performing seal. 'That is excellent, very well done, Alice. I think the combination of therapy and medication is perfect for you. I said exactly that to Dr Barnes when we last discussed your case.'

I wasn't taking the medication. I hid the tablets under my tongue and then spat them out. I was thinking, *Fuck the psychiatrist and fuck you, too.* But things appeared to be going my way, as I'd hoped, as I'd planned. At the end of our one-hour session, Dr Sandler offered to lend me a book. The true story of a convicted murderer who had gone on to do charity work years later. I held the book up in front of me, reading the blurb on the back cover – another opportunity to pull her strings.

'Thank you, doctor, it looks both inspirational and inspiring. I'd *love* to read it.'

'That's good, Alice, I feel sure you'll find it interesting.'

I stood to leave as the clock reached 4pm, the paperback held in one hand. I was trembling slightly and sweating too. That wasn't an act. But I hoped it would serve me well.

'There is one other thing I'd like to mention, doctor. I've

been putting it off, but I think now's the time. It'll be too late if I don't ask you today.'

'Okay, I, er, I think I know what this is about. But, come on, no assumptions. You need to say it for yourself.'

I nodded and then wiped the sweat from my brow. 'I would *really* appreciate the opportunity to attend my mother's funeral. Have you had a chance to talk to Dr Barnes?'

Then the words I was desperate to hear. 'I can't make any promises, Alice. But it's looking hopeful. I'll see what I can do.'

41

D r Sandler waved to me from the hospital canteen's serving counter as I sat alone at lunchtime the following day. She looked as self-satisfied as a butcher's dog as she approached me, weaving between the tables with a cup of hot soup held in one hand. My odious father tried to plant doubts in my mind with his usual moronic chatter. But the psychologist's face told its own happy story. I knew it was going to be good news even before she joined me at the table.

'I was hoping to catch you, Alice.'

She always used my name. It was Alice this and Alice that. As if she needed to remind me who I was. I sat in silence, waiting for her to continue as I knew she inevitably would. She looked at me over the top of her metal-rimmed glasses.

'I've, er, I've been discussing your case with Dr Barnes. It wasn't an easy decision given your offending history. But you'll no doubt be delighted to hear that he's agreed to you attending your mother's funeral service.'

'Oh, that's *wonderful*! Thank you so very much.'

Her expression became more serious. 'I'm glad you're pleased. But there are caveats. You'll be attending the cremation but not the church service. I hope you can accept that compromise.'

I put my knife and fork down, my meal half-eaten. 'I'm grateful, it's marvellous news, but why the conditions?'

'The church is in a busy town, and the crematorium in the countryside. Fewer people means less attention. It's that simple.'

I nodded. 'Okay, I understand.'

'And there's something else. You won't be going alone. I'll be travelling with you, and so will one of the male nurses. He'll be doing the driving. And you won't be left alone at any time during the day. We'll travel to Wales early in the morning and then return as soon as the service is over.'

It wasn't perfect. Escape wouldn't be easy. But I had a plan in mind. And that was a lot better than nothing.

'Thank you, doctor. I very much appreciate everything you've done for me.'

And I meant it too. Just not in the way the stupid bitch thought.

42

We began our journey to Wales as the hint of the day to come lit the sky at the horizon. I had my manuscript under my clothes, tucked into the waistband of my trousers. We were all dressed in black, even the nurse, whom I saw without his hospital uniform for the first time. It wasn't exactly the best start to the day. The nurse reminded me of my father. But I forced the poisonous rodent from my mind. I had to focus on escape. The trip was my only chance. I felt sure of that. There was no room for distractions.

The nurse did the driving while Dr Sandler and I sat in the back with our shoulders almost touching. She talked at me incessantly during the journey, spouting some mindless crap or other until I was close to exploding. And my purgatory got even worse as we crossed the Severn Bridge towards the Welsh border. I had the psychologist chattering in one ear and my father in the other getting louder and louder as I attempted to ignore him. I wanted to scream until all was silence. But I somehow held my battered emotions in check by focusing on the end game. It would have felt so delicious to elbow Dr

Sandler in the mouth; to ram her yellow teeth down her snaky throat with either fist. But the time wasn't right for violence. There was a bigger picture to consider. And so I did my best to ignore her too.

I exchanged friendly hand gestures with my grandmother and sister as we entered the crematorium's carefully manicured grounds after a four-hour journey. I noted the position of my grandmother's car as the nurse pulled up at the far side of the car park, well away from other vehicles, as if I had some contagious disease that couldn't be cured. I looked around me as the three of us walked towards my relatives, Dr Sandler immediately next to me and the nurse close behind.

The crematorium's gardens reminded me of my rose garden, bringing a tear to my eye. But I told myself to focus. I was there for a reason and had to keep that at the forefront of my mind.

I hugged my sister first, and then my gran, who whispered in my ear, 'It's all done.'

I met her eyes, our noses virtually touching, and smiled in response. I didn't say anything for fear of being overheard, as the hearse made its way towards us, stopping immediately opposite the main entrance a few feet from where we were standing.

I felt everyone's eyes on me as we sat at the front of the crematorium's small chapel minutes later as if they were attempting to penetrate my soul. I wanted to yell, to shout, to beat them to a pulp, but I sat there in silence with my relatives to one side of me and my supervisors to the other. I glanced around me, surveying the scene. A priest stood in the pulpit almost directly opposite me. My mother's coffin festooned in flowers sat on a series of rollers I can only assume led to the furnace. And there were two doors, the one through which we'd entered behind me and another smaller one to my immediate right. I decided that the smaller of the two doors was the most suitable when I made my move. I only hoped Dr Sandler would come to the same conclusion.

I listened with my nerves in shreds as the priest welcomed all those in attendance, explaining the nature of the service as if it wasn't blatantly obvious to everyone.

As the first hymn began, I stood on shaky legs, squeezing Dr Sandler's hand, gaining her attention, before whispering in her ear. 'I'm sorry, doctor, I need the toilet.'

She frowned hard, the order of service in one hand. 'Really? Now? Can't it wait?'

I lowered my voice to a whisper. My mouth felt so very parched. The words almost stuck in my throat. 'It's urgent, my, er, my period has started.'

She gave me a sympathetic look, screwing up her face before speaking to the nurse in a low voice. He nodded twice as she took my arm, leading me into the aisle and through the door to our right as everyone else continued singing. A minute later, we were out of the chapel room and entering a small toilet block with a restricted car park view. To my relief, the male nurse hadn't followed us.

As the psychologist reached into her handbag for a sanitary towel, I drew my head back and butted her hard, bang, right on the bridge of her nose.

As she staggered backwards with blood running from both nostrils, I followed my initial assault with a powerful punch to her throat, preventing her from shouting out or screaming. As she fell to the floor, I leapt on top of her, raining down punch after powerful punch until sure she was unconscious. I washed the blood from my hands, searched her bag, took her cash, threw her phone into the toilet bowl, and then headed for the car park at a fast walking pace. I was tempted to run, but I feared it might draw the attention of anyone who happened to be passing on the nearby road.

My heart was pounding as I jumped into the driver's seat of my grandmother's four-door saloon, finding the keys in the glovebox as she'd promised. I looked back as I drove toward the exit, but there was nothing to see. It seemed the service was continuing without us. Now all I had to do was keep moving.

43

A police car sped past me in the opposite direction about ten minutes or so after I'd left the crematorium's grounds on my way to the ferry port of Fishguard in the north of the county. I pulled into an off-road café popular with truck drivers, hid the car from passers-by behind a substantial articulated lorry, and retrieved a rucksack from the boot.

As promised by my grandmother, it contained a change of clothes, a good quality blonde shoulder-length wig, and £3,000 cash in used notes. I hurriedly changed in the back seat of the car, entered the café, enjoying a quick fry-up before finally persuading the third of three Ireland-bound lorry drivers to give me a lift as far as Rosslare, hiding me in the back amongst the cargo as we crossed the borders.

The middle-aged fat man was reluctant at first, much like the first two drivers who'd refused to help out of hand. But the combined offer of £500 cash and oral sex changed the fat man's mind pretty quickly. I picked up a steak knife as I followed him towards his vehicle, dropping it into my rucksack before putting the bag on my back.

Five hours later and I found myself in Ireland, as the driver opened the lorry's rear doors with a hungry leer on his face. He gave up on the idea of a blow job pretty quickly when I held the point of the knife to his throat. He even returned my money, which I happily took, thinking it would come in useful. I considered killing him for his conduct but decided against. I'm not sure why. Maybe it was because I didn't have time for a trial. And so I just slashed his face to mark him as a danger forever before jumping from the rear of the truck and leaving the area as fast as my feet could carry me.

I booked into a cheap guest house close to the harbour, gaining work as a cleaner two days later. By then I had a new look, a new name, and, I like to think, a pretty convincing new accent which I won't disclose. I watched the local news and read the local papers, but there were no reports of my escape. My father knew I was there, of course. I can't escape that bastard. But no one else seemed interested. I kept a close eye out for the police for weeks after that, but nobody came. Gradually I began to relax. It appeared my plan had worked even better than I could have hoped.

That was a little over six months ago now. I've since moved on again, working as a ship's cook with no questions asked. We travelled to mainland Europe first, and then on from there. I won't reveal my location at the time of writing my final chapter. The reasons for that should be evident to anyone. I'll tell you that I'm safe somewhere in the world, and you'll have to be satisfied with that.

I considered destroying my manuscript more than once during the writing, despite my initial enthusiasm. I came to the realisation that I gave away too many clues as to my identity and location. But that no longer matters. It's of no consequence. No one's going to find me. So here it is.

I plan to return to Wales one fine day when I think it's safe to do so. There are other monsters out there. Beasts I'll hunt again when I get the chance. It will happen, but I can't tell you when, that's in the lap of the gods. Only time will tell.

THE END

A NOTE FROM THE PUBLISHER

Thank you for reading this book. If you enjoyed it please do consider leaving a review on Amazon to help others find it too.

We hate typos. All of our books have been rigorously edited and proofread, but sometimes mistakes do slip through. If you have spotted a typo, please do let us know and we can get it amended within hours.

info@bloodhoundbooks.com

Printed in Great Britain
by Amazon